The Black Walrus

Joseph Caldara

Silver Moose Press

AURORA, COLORADO

Silver Moose Press
Aurora, Colorado 80017
www.josephcaldaraauthor.com

Publisher's Note: This is a work of fiction. Names, characters, places, and incidents are a product of the author's imagination. Locales and public names are sometimes used for atmospheric purposes. Any resemblance to actual people, living or dead, or to events, institutions, or locales is completely coincidental. Names of companies and branded products are used within the bounds of copyright law and fair use. Brand and company names used in this work include Charmin®, Pepto Bismol®, Rhoomba®, Buick®, Jello®, Steak-Umm®, Smurf®, The Young and the Restless®, Chiquita®, Nair®, Riverdance®, Cheeto®, Neapolitan®, Cadbury Egg®, Disney®, Bengay®, Bobblehead®, Listerine®, Zamboni®, Jetski®, The Matrix®, Super Friends®, Rogaine®, Captain Underpants®, Redwall®, and The Lord of the Rings®. Publisher does not claim ownership of any mentioned brands or products.

Cover Design © 2023 by Joseph Caldara and Silver Moose Press, L.L.C. Cover produced by Nathan Dasco. Cover illustrations produced by Abigail Chrystine.

Book Layout © 2017 BookDesignTemplates.com

Edited by Paula Silici

Beta Readers: Ezra James Ahlberg, Zia Leonard, Carson McCarty

RMFW Aurora Critique Group: Anita Meyer Bunten, Karen Call, John M. Campbell, Mindy Kinnaman, Donna Lawrence, Fran Scannell, Roebrt Selzer, Natli VanDerWerken, Authors

Special Thanks to: God, Cathy Humphreys, Steve Caldara, and all AuthorYOU staff and members

The Black Walrus/ Joseph Caldara. -- First edition
ISBN Number (Ingram Spark): 978-0-9984298-6-1
ISBN Number (Print): 978-0-9984298-8-5
ISBN Number (eBook): 978-0-9984298-7-8
Library of Congress Control Number: 2023904750

Dedication

To Grandpa

Who encouraged and inspired me to push my
imagination to its limit and to laugh always.

CONTENTS

Chapter 1

Alex yanked open the door to his locker and threw his hands up, bracing himself. The mountain of paper teetered like a cartoon stack of pancakes about to fall, and Alex leaned against it with his shoulder like he was trying to body-check a staggering brown bear.

He dug through the mountain of notebook paper and comic books with his free hand. Some of the pages slipped out of the main clump and floated to the tile floor. Alex glanced at each scribbled drawing, keeping track of the pieces of paper he'd need to pick up after he found what he was looking for.

There were the plans for the grappling hook guns that still needed a propulsion system and the blueprints for the miniaturized smoke bombs and the pages and pages he'd dedicated to

1

finding a way to build an interspecies communication system.

At last, he found it: a moist, room-temperature, half-eaten carton of tapioca pudding sandwiched between a few empty cans of Caffeine Armageddon energy drink and an old issue of *The Inexplicable Mullet Man*.

Alex didn't really like tapioca, but he'd found that it had the best weight balance of all the puddings. It was firm, yet slick enough to get the job done. Like a 1920s bootlegger or Charmin ultra-absorb toilet paper.

"Hi, Alex!" Alex turned his head to face Tracy Stranson. She was twirling her curly blond hair and smacking her lips as she chewed some gum, probably her thirtieth stick today. "Were you lost in your own, little world again?" Tracy giggled.

Alex shoved the mound of paper back inside his locker and scooped the scattered sheets off the floor. The familiar sights and smells of Cremini City Middle School returned to him.

Sneakers squeaked and slapped on the tile floor while hundreds of chattering voices merged together into an indecipherable din. It was cool; the air conditioner was always cranked up too high.

"Yes," he said, "I was pondering the viability of some new crime-fighting devices. Nothing you'd be interested in."

Alex tried his best to avoid eye contact with anyone, even students he knew. Eye contact might mean getting sucked into a conversation about a geometry test or the next school dance or the latest sports ball game or why you shouldn't soak your feet in Pepto Bismol, despite its skin-moistening effects. There was no time for such pleasantries.

"How do you know I wouldn't be interested?" Tracy snapped through gum-smacks. "You're so quiet and weird. I was just trying to be friendly."

"Well, so was that guy who threw his neighbor's dirty poodle in a washing machine."

"What are you doing with that pudding? It smells and it looks way too old to—"

"Shh!" Alex raised his hand and put a finger in front of Tracy's mouth, "It's 1:43pm. It won't be long before Brandon walks through this hallway."

Alex spotted Drew Patterson across the hall. Drew was new to Cremini City and didn't have many friends. He wasn't the sharpest quill at the porcupine convention, either. Before Drew, Alex had never heard anyone try to spell "ketchup" with numbers, emoticons, or Egyptian hieroglyphics.

Sure enough, Alex caught a glimpse of Brandon Spiko strutting down the hallway. He was fingering a smartphone in a case covered with cartoon penguins, a phone Alex was sure he'd acquired just minutes ago.

None of the bigger students seemed to notice or care. This was Cremini City, after all. Theft wasn't exactly a rare occurrence.

"Why do you want anything to do with Brandon?" Tracy asked, clinging closer to the lockers and lowering her voice to a whisper as she placed her hand on Alex's shoulder.

The chatter grew quiet as Brandon walked down the hallway. "You saw what he did to Keith last week, and I hear he almost joined the Birthday Gang." She shivered. "Alex, I think this could get ugly. You aren't going to pick a fight, are you?"

Brandon shoved the phone into one of the pockets of his leather jacket and slicked his hair back. Each student Brandon came near hopped out of his way like a frightened gazelle.

Alex made a fist and gritted his teeth. He studied Brandon carefully as the red-haired menace stuck out his right leg and tripped another student. Brandon's eyes were locked on Drew like a lion stalking its prey.

Alex had to act quickly.

He surveyed the hallway, making sure no one was watching him. Like a shuffleboard player preparing his shot, Alex placed the tapioca pudding cup in front of the toe of his shoe. Shoving the cup just a little, he sent it skidding across the hallway like a hockey puck. It stopped just in front of Brandon.

Alex spun to the right and marched toward room 38 for his science class, keeping his back to the crowd in the hallway. He heard the satisfying smack of boy-against-tile. Brandon spewed swear words like a sailor with a scorpion in his pants as Drew bolted past. Alex grinned.

* * *

Alex took his seat near the back of the class and set a piece of loose-leaf paper and his copy of "The Ecology of the South American Rainforest" on the desk. He opened it to a random page—it didn't matter which one he turned to; he'd finished the book and completed all the homework assignments months ago—and scanned the classroom, looking for Ms. Grunderson. The other students filed in and slid into their seats.

Alex spotted a girl texting furiously. Her eyes grew wider, and her mouth curled into a smile as she tapped the phone screen like each finger was a tiny woodpecker.

Alex wondered who she was texting and what she was getting so excited about. In fact, he thought, wouldn't it be fascinating if he could somehow ... construct some sort of device that would ... allow him to ....

Alex grabbed the piece of paper and began scribbling with the excitement of a shih tzu discovering a mountain made of bacon. It would have to be small, able to be concealed in a piece of clothing. There would have to be an antenna, something about the width of a yak's hair, that could transmit to an earpiece.

It'd need to be attached to a device capable of intercepting and deciphering cell phone and radio signals. Then he'd be able to use police radio signals to pinpoint crimes in progress. And if he could find a way to suit up in just a few seconds—

"Alex Portobello!"

Alex's head shot up, and his glasses jiggled. Above him loomed the gray-haired, jowly, scowling face of Ms. Grunderson. She snatched the piece of notebook paper and examined it.

"'Communications interceptor for use in crime-fighting arsenal'," she read aloud. Dipping her head and narrowing her eyes, she sighed. "Alex, this drawing doesn't have anything to do with our current discussion on the ecosystem of the South American rainforest, does it?"

"I suppose not," Alex said, "But you'll find that the design is mechanically sound. This *is* a science class, isn't it?"

"Yes. But we're studying biomes right now. I've told you before: you can work on your drawings on your own time."

"But Ms. Grunderson, if I finish my arsenal, all I'll need is a colorful crime-fighting uniform and I could finally be a ... be a ... something ... more than a plain, old student."

"I see. Well, for failing to pay attention, I'm giving you an extra assignment: you are to write a five-page essay about the appearance and properties of each of the seventeen South American rainforest plants we've discussed and their effect on the ecosystem. And you'll be presenting it to the class tomorrow."

Alex straightened his mouth as Ms. Grunderson walked away and continued her lecture. "That ecosystem must be impressive if it can come close to matching your effect on a biome," he mumbled. He got a snicker from the seat behind him.

Chapter 2

In a dark, foreboding laboratory on the other side of Cremini City, boiling chemicals burbled in their test tubes. Electric currents surged through cylindrical analyzers, buzzing as they arced from one end of the machines to the other. A hundred flashing lights illuminated the dark laboratory, and in the middle of the lab, an elephant-sized view screen hummed.

Floofles, the lab's resident Chihuahua, yipped at what looked like a gaggle of Roombas skittering across the floor, each with a metallic, mechanical arm jutting from its back. Some of them carried wrenches and screwdrivers, others tiny cups of strong coffee.

Against the lab's west wall, in front of the giant monitor, Dr. Filbert Thorium cackled with excitement. "It's nearly finished," the scientist exclaimed, rubbing his hands together with his eyes transfixed on the view screen.

On the screen, Thorium could see an ordinary, suburban household. The Portobello household. Bubbling and humming sounds came from the kitchen as a woman prepared a pot of beef stew.

The tiny camera Dr. Thorium used to spy on his test subject was positioned in the living room and angled so he could see through the open doorway into the kitchen.

His view of the kitchen was obstructed, but he could see the back door clearly. The young man who lived here always came in through the back door. And Dr. Thorium had big plans in store for his test subject: thirteen-year-old Alex Portobello.

Thorium picked up his Chihuahua and held it just an inch from his face. "Just think of it, Floofles," he whispered to his furry companion, "my greatest creation, nearly complete! Today, we learn of the energy core's full effect on human tissue."

Floofles let out a tiny growl. The office chair squeaked as Thorium leaned back, trying not to break visual contact with the squirming, little dog as he imagined the device's potential.

"Provided I got the radiation levels on the energy core right, the possibilities are endless. We could grow tomatoes the size of Buicks— world hunger solved! We could rub the core on tree bark and affect the plant's very cellular structure—it'd make the best maple syrup you've ever tasted! We could expose grass to it and feed the grass to cows—think of the manure quality, Floofles, the manure quality!"

Dr. Thorium turned his attention to the view screen once again. At 3:47 p.m. precisely (the boy always got home at 3:47), Thorium watched as the back door of the Portobello house opened and a skinny, brown-haired boy with round glasses and a Robo-Alpaca Versus Ninjapottomus t-shirt tramped in.

His shoulders were slumped, which Dr. Thorium had learned meant someone had insulted his designs again.

"Hi, sweetie." the woman's voice came over the view screen's speakers. She hugged the boy's side and let out a sigh of relief at seeing her son home safe. "How was school today?"

"It was fantastic, Mom. I was perfecting scientific marvels in science class and, as punishment, have to write a five-page essay about plants."

Dr. Thorium turned up the volume on his monitor so he could better hear the conversation. The woman released her son. "Alex, how many times have we talked about this? You need to learn how to communicate with other people. And you need to come back down to reality sometimes. You can't keep disrupting class."

"I wasn't the one who disrupted it. I don't understand, Mom. When I get an idea for a new device, something just snaps, and I feel like I have Mexican jumping beans in my fingers and dozens of prairie dogs tap dancing in my brain. And it's getting harder to control. I just have to keep designing machinery and perfecting my martial art. So I'll be prepared."

"Prepared for what?"

"Uh ... prepared for ... the comic convention ... next month. I want to make a costume."

"Ookay ...." The boy's mother crossed her arms and raised an eyebrow. "Well ... your dad will be home soon, and dinner will be ready in about half an hour. Maybe you should go 'prepare' for that."

As he watched Alex trudge out of the kitchen and climb the stairs, Dr. Thorium giggled until his stomach hurt. He thought back to that summer five years ago, the day he'd snuck into the electronics store with the energy core and a miniature camera. He'd felt discouraged that day, the day after his meeting with Gigantocorp's corporate bigwigs, the ones who funded his research.

Dr. Thorium snatched a cup of coffee from one of the floor robots and swallowed it in one swig. He wasn't a "mad scientist" or "evil genius" or anything like that. But it was imperative he test the effects of the core's radiation on human tissue.

He'd wanted to test the effects of the energy core's radiation on himself, not to harm anyone else. Of course, the board had given him a firm "no."

So naturally, he'd done what any dejected scientist would do: he broke into an electronics store under the cover of darkness, disassembled a television, secured the energy core inside it, and attached a video camera to the outside.

While he reminisced, Thorium ran his fingers across the bright red "TL" logo on his customized lab coat ("TL" stood for "Thorium Laboratories.")

Eventually, someone had bought the television and installed it in his living room, and Thorium met his test subject: eight-year-old Alex Portobello. Alex used the television more than his parents did; he liked cartoons, video games, documentaries about the mating rituals of naked mole rats—typical kid's stuff. And despite his mother's warnings, he sat too close to the TV. Way too close.

As the months passed, the perfectly-normal, ethical scientist noticed a subtle change in the young boy he'd exposed to a radioactive isotope. Alex's speech became more intelligent and he started … designing things.

At first, it'd been little inventions like a spoon holder made of Tinker Toys that was supposed to make it easier to eat cereal (it didn't.) But after a year or two, Alex began drawing up designs for jet-propelled foot massagers and ferret-powered ray guns.

Thorium scratched Floofles behind the ears. "Tonight we flip the switch, little friend. It's time to turn the energy core's radiation to full power.

Who knows what the boy will be able to accomplish when we unchain his potential ... provided his cerebellum doesn't melt like butter in a volcano, of course. I mean, it won't. I'm pretty sure. I'm 73% sure, at least."

Chapter 3

A squeaky thud echoed throughout the dimly lit bedroom as Alex punched his inflatable replica of superstar singer Spanky St. Jivestrunky between the eyes. It popped up, ready for another hit. Another afternoon of training.

He'd tried blow-up, wobbling punching bags of other animals and personalities—a penguin in a jogging suit, local newscaster Max Blatherson, trailblazing microbiologist and flamenco dancer Stephanie Booperstein—but he found that Jivestrunky's face offered a perfect target: it was firm, but with a little give.

Alex stood in the only available patch of floor in the small, darkened room. His bed was wedged against the wall. As he tossed his phone onto the bed, the folds of the thrown-together sheets and green blanket seemed to swallow it like a giant frog.

Alex always tossed his cell phone onto the bed right after school so it wouldn't interfere with his martial arts practice. He'd cleared the part of the floor where he kept his inflatable punching bags, but the rest of the floor was covered in gears and sheets of paper, detached nail gun triggers, empty metallic capsules, and other things Alex had picked up from the Internet or the dumpster behind the mechanic's shop.

Alex's computer desk was just as messy. The area that held the monitor and keyboard were clear, but the rest of the desk was covered in pieces of notebook paper, and occasionally, one would drift to the floor.

He'd tried to keep the computer tower itself clean to keep it cool, but he hadn't. Alex had plastered the tower with the stickers he'd gotten from the premiere of *Mullet Man vs. The Living Baklava*, but he could barely see them under the dust.

As soon as he noticed the computer monitor was on, Alex darted across the room to turn it off. On the monitor was the footage from each of his security cameras.

In one corner of the screen was a window showing the area just outside the front door, while other cameras revealed the back yard, the side yard with the gate, his bedroom, the living room, the kitchen, Alex's special guinea pig triathlete training facility and microwave-sized steam room in the basement, and the rest of the house.

Alex's parents had told him to take down the cameras months ago. They said the security system was "creepy" and "unnecessary" and "a violation of both HOA policy and a disturbing window into the goings-on of that raccoon that lives beneath the shed." But he'd kept the cameras up anyway.

Once his crime-fighting arsenal was ready, Alex planned to watch over his house like a half-starved badger over a swimming pool full of Steak-Ummms.

He returned to the other side of the room to resume his fight against the inflatable punching bag. Just a few more maneuvers and he'd have a new move to add to his martial art. He punched the balloon again, delivering two swift blows, one to the right cheek and one just below the chin.

Ducking out of instinct—he had to be ready for whatever an opponent could throw at him— Alex squatted and delivered a kick to Jivestrunky's midsection. The whine of escaping air told Alex he'd done some real damage.

Hopping to his feet, he ran to the desk and rifled through the drawers. He had an army of pencils and pens, but the drawers mostly contained mound after mound of blank notebook paper, scribbled drawings, and comic books. Alex dug a roll of duct tape out of the desk, pumped more air into the balloon, and patched it up. Jivestrunky was ready for another bout.

He snatched a pencil and bounded to the opposite wall. Scanning the wall for the right piece of paper made Alex realize that perhaps Mom was right: his bedroom walls were a bit of a mess.

There were countless pieces of loose-leaf notebook paper he'd jammed onto the walls with thumb tacks alongside the posters featuring Mullet Man and Legume Woman and Captain Short Shorts and the rest of Alex's favorite characters. Alex couldn't even remember what color his bedroom walls were painted.

At last, he found what he was looking for: a sheet of paper featuring stick figures drawn in different positions. Carefully, Alex drew another series of figures that mimicked the moves he'd just performed on the Jivestrunky balloon. He nodded. More moves to add to his martial art.

"Whatcha doing, son? Adding some more art to your wall?"

Alex jumped a little and turned to face his dad. Dad had changed out of his work clothes and put on his t-shirt from the family's trip to the Grand Canyon. His hair was still perfectly combed, like a field of wheat viewed from a helicopter.

"Hey, Dad." Alex smiled. "I'm glad you arrived home without incident. Yeah, I was just adding some more decorations to my wall. You know how concerned we kids are these days with being trendy and dapper."

"Yeah, I'll bet that's it." Alex's dad took a step into the room and gave his son a quick hug.

"I wish you wouldn't worry about whether I'm going to get home safely. Downtown Cremini City isn't exactly a field of lilacs, but I know which alleys to avoid. Besides, we have something else to talk about. Your mom told me what happened: you ruffled your teacher's feathers."

"What?"

"You got ol' Ms. Grunderson's goat. You rustled her jimmies. You jostled her smurfs. You drove a taxi through her chinchilla patch is what you did."

"I believe jostling smurfs is illegal in this part of the country, Dad."

Alex's dad sat on the bed and motioned for his son to sit next to him. "So what are you really up to, son?"

"Oh, you know … just, uh … organizing my comic books and … getting ready to write about rainforest plants."

"Son, you've spent the last few months designing hand-held gadgets and developing your own martial arts style. You really think your mother and I can't see what you're trying to do?"

Alex cleared his throat. "What are you babbling about, Dad? I'm just fascinated by science and really old things from Asia, that's all.

Why do you think I made all those macaroni sculptures of Emperor Qin Shi Huang?"

Walt Portobello placed his hand on his son's shoulder. "It's fine to have interests, son. But you might be taking the costumed hero thing a little too far. A boy your age ought to be out catching frogs down at the creek with his buddies or chasing girls or poking dead squirrels."

"I don't have a lot of 'buddies,' Dad. And those buddies I do have know how important it is for me to prioritize my projects over social engagements. But I still value my friendships."

Alex's phone started buzzing, and the smooth, groovy sounds of Johnny Meatball and the Porkettes' smash hit "Gotta Find Me a Jello-Lovin' Woman" erupted from it. He picked up the phone and looked at the screen.

"Brian's calling, Dad. I asked him to help me with an experiment this afternoon. If he hasn't puked by now, then we'll know properly-aged toe jam is a viable mustard substitute!"

Walt Portobello sighed through his nose and lowered his head, running his fingers across his temples. "You like living in Cremini City, don't you, Alex?" he said, turning to his son once again.

"Absolutely. We've always lived here."

"Okay. And I know you know it's not the safest place for people who spend too much time up in their heads, in their own little world. They sometimes get mugged. Or worse."

"Yes, Dad. I know," Alex groaned.

"And we've already talked about what's going to happen if you don't improve your behavior and start paying more attention. We can't afford to move, and we can't just let you keep disrespecting your teachers and walking home from school by yourself when you're so detached from reality. But your GPA's so good, I know you could get a scholarship to—"

"I know, Dad. Colonel Primpington's Boarding School for Wayward Youngsters." Alex shivered. His dad had insisted they visit the school during their trip to Misery Bay, Michigan. To Alex, that place seemed more like a prison than a school.

He'd watched uniformed students without a hair out of place march wordlessly across the sterile campus under the watchful eyes of the school disciplinarians who stood on every corner.

The classroom Alex and his parents had visited had a big poster with a giant, smiling honey bee with a bow tie that said "Suppression of one's individuality is the bee's knees!"

That huge bee seemed to scowl down at the students, who sat in class motionless with their hands folded, their eyes darting from the tops of their desks to their dictatorial teachers and back again. The whole thing reminded Alex of some dystopian, sci-fi movie.

But the school's classes and campus were nothing compared to what Alex would lose if his parents shipped him off to boarding school.

He'd lose his bedroom and everything in it. There were no comic books or self-taught martial arts allowed at Colonel Primpington's, and they certainly wouldn't tolerate any "gadgets" or "inventing."

Worst of all, if Alex went to boarding school, his parents and classmates would be alone in Cremini City, at the mercy of the Birthday Gang and the other ne'er-do-wells who ran rampant. His crime-fighting gadgets, his hand-to-hand combat repertoire, his jet-powered go-go boots … all of it would be useless to protect them.

"You've already got one strike against you, son. You remember that talk we had: three strikes and we'll have no choice but to send you to Colonel Primpington's."

"Okay, Dad," Alex said, swallowing the lump in his throat, "I'll try to be more respectful and ... present, I guess."

Dad gave Alex a pat on the back and stood, walking to the bedroom door. "Thanks, son. Think about what I said, and try to communicate a little better with your teachers and classmates. That's all we're asking of you. Dinner's almost ready. Wash up and come downstairs soon.

"Oh," Alex's dad turned his head, "And remember, your mother and I are going to the Porkstons' to play bridge on Thursday night. Will you be all right by yourself while we're gone?"

Alex perked his head up. That's right! He'd be home alone this Thursday. "Yesssss," Alex said, fighting the grin that began to spread across his face.

Dad crossed his arms. "Are you sure? I don't want a repeat of last time we left you by yourself. You know, we never did get those grape jelly stains out of the carpet. And I never want to hear a fumigator utter the phrase 'lingering manatee stench' again."

"I promise I won't do anything out of the ordinary, Dad," said Alex as his dad walked out of the bedroom. He knew he could keep his word to his parents and still have fun Thursday night. After all, there were all kinds of things that fit within Alex's definition of "ordinary."

Chapter 4

Miles away, in a small shopping center near downtown Cremini City, narrow rays of sunlight streaked across the wooden floor of Reggie's Grocery.

Stevia Brinkles ran her fingers across the dozens of pickle jars, searching for Uncle Shnoofin's Feel-Good Crunchy Dills. The pickles were at the end of an aisle near the front of the store, which made it easy for Stevia to see both the aisles and Reggie, the owner, standing at the cash register.

Aisles of delicious food lined the main floor of the store, and brightly colored, hand-painted signs told customers where to find the things they wanted.

The place smelled of meat, crackers, twenty-seven different cheeses, and the three-day-old flowers in the floral section that had begun to wilt. The florescent lights buzzed, and faintly, the freezer hummed.

There weren't many customers, but it was a homey kind of place, which was just the way both Stevia and Reggie liked it. As Stevia scanned the tops of the aisles, she heard the sound of flicking paper and smiled. Mrs. Poodleman was thumbing through the tabloids again.

"Reggie!" Mrs. Poodleman shouted across the store, "D'jyou hear Dracula joined the navy again? And he's dating the Chiquita banana lady."

"Is that right, Mrs. P?" Reggie said, scratching his mustache. Stevia rolled her eyes. She didn't have the heart to tell Mrs. Poodleman it was all a bunch of bunk.

After all, everyone knew Dracula was still in a blissful, monogamous relationship with that bear from the detergent commercials.

A tiny bell rang. Stevia turned, and Reggie opened his arms to welcome a new customer. But his smile dropped. He turned pale.

A man stepped into his shop wearing a long, brown overcoat and a matching fedora tilted downward to obscure his face. His shoes clacked against the floor as he walked straight toward the counter.

Stevia shifted closer to the pickle shelf, hoping the newcomer wouldn't see her. She didn't need to get a better look at the guy to figure out who this was. Everybody in Cremini City knew.

Felix's usual crew filed into the shop behind him. First came Gary, a short, weasely-looking man fingering with a sharp cake knife. His shirt was ripped near the shoulder, but his purple, pointed party hat looked as bright as ever.

Next came a big guy carrying a piñata. Even though he wore a blindfold, he had no trouble finding his way around the shop. Stevia felt him wink at her through the silk barrier covering his eyes. She shuddered.

Three or four other guys came in carrying colorfully wrapped presents, noisemakers, streamers, and plates of decorative cake. The man in the fedora cocked his head, and his companions broke formation, dashing around Reggie's store and stuffing their pockets with anything they could carry.

As one of the ruffians bolted past her, Stevia put her hands up, keeping the pickle jars from falling. The blindfolded guy with the piñata stayed at the front of the store with his leader.

Finally, Felix reached the counter.

"Afternoon, Reggie," he said, lifting the brim of his hat and placing the palm of his other hand on the countertop. The man's face was smooth and handsome.

"Felix Cumpleaños," Reggie said, leaning back and folding his arms. "To what do I owe the pleasure?"

"Well, I hate to be a pain, but I've come concerning your payment." Felix stretched out his hand toward the shop owner.

Stevia heard a jelly jar smash against the floor. She could almost smell the sweat beading on Reggie's neck. "I told you: business has been slow lately."

"Business was slow last week. And the week before that. I'm losing my patience, Reggie. I've got bills to pay, too, you know. It's not easy offering protection services to so many ... vulnerable clients."

Felix peeled back his lips and smiled as the sound of boxes being ripped open and fruit splatting against the walls echoed through the store. Stevia heard someone shatter the freezer door. "I'd hate for something to happen to your lovely little shop," Felix sneered.

Reggie quivered, but he kept standing up straight. Hardening his gaze, he looked Felix straight in the eyes. In response, Felix gestured with his arm toward Stevia. Both Reggie and Felix looked down the aisle as the muscular man with the piñata strode toward her.

Stevia took a step back, then froze, as a wave of goosebumps crept over her.

Grasping the side of his papier-mâché donkey, the man grabbed a metal handle and pulled it back. The piñata made a sha-shack sound like the cocking of a candy-filled gun.

"All right," Reggie moaned, clenching his eyes shut and opening the cash register. He pulled out a wad of cash, counted it, and slapped it into Felix Cumpleaños' outstretched hand.

Felix snapped his fingers. The blindfolded man lowered his piñata, and all of Felix's goons staggered out the door. "Always nice doing business with you, Reg."

Reggie shook his head, closed the register, and trudged toward the maintenance closet to grab a broom. Stevia finally let loose the breath she'd been holding in and made a fist, cursing the air.

There was no point in her calling the police. By the time they arrived, Felix and his henchmen would be long gone.

* * *

The man in the cone-shaped hat sighed as he popped open a stolen soda. "Something wrong, Gary?" Felix asked, stuffing the cash into his pocket.

"Don't you think we might be going a little too far, boss? We just threatened someone in broad daylight." Gary took a swig. "What if, you know, the cops had shown up?"

Felix laughed as he bit into a stolen beef jerky stick. "Cops? We've got them running scared, Gary. And who else'll get in our way? Ain't nobody in Cremini City dumb enough to mess with the Birthday Gang."

Chapter 5

"The Amazon rainforest contains a variety of animal and plant life, including the rubber tree and heliconia flower. Each of these plants contributes to the tropical, temperate ecosystem of the rainforest in a unique way and—"

Alex dropped his pencil and groaned. His downtrodden buttocks sank into the brown, leather couch. The TV bathed the living room in a bluish light. The couch, recliner, and potted fichus plant that sat on an end table cast shadows across the closed blinds.

Alex's bedroom was just up the stairs, directly above the living room, so it'd been easy for him to sneak down the stairs after his parents went to bed.

He liked to do his schoolwork in front of the TV. The noise helped to quiet some of the more … creative parts of his brain.

It was late. Alex had meant to finish his essay during the afternoon, but he'd had some more ideas for his fighting style and then had this itch to build smoke bombs and then had a spark of inspiration for the propulsion system of his grapple guns and ... before he knew it, he was stuck piecing together a plant essay in the middle of the night.

"The walrus spends approximately half its life in the water," the voice on the TV droned in a tone just soft enough that it wouldn't wake Alex's parents, "where it searches for mussels, clams, and the other bottom-dwelling shellfish that make up its primary source of food. The walrus' tusks are elongated canine teeth and are used to puncture holes in the ice, making it easier for it to climb out of the water."

Alex massaged his forehead and sighed. He shifted his legs onto the couch's armrest and stretched out. Maybe the muse of plant essays would strike if he lay down.

* * *

Hands quivering, Dr. Thorium gripped the lever on the control panel and eased it downward, increasing the intensity of the energy core's radiation. The buzzing of the lab's electrical devices and bubbling of the test tubes had ceased for the day, leaving the lab silent.

Thorium drummed the table with the fingers on his left hand and stared at the viewscreen, which displayed a reclining Alex Portobello. Even Floofles had stopped his usual barking and whining and stared at the viewscreen, his tiny Chihuahua nose whistling as he breathed.

* * *

"The walrus uses its sensitive whiskers, known as vibrissae, to detect sources of food while underwater."

Alex was staring at the ceiling now. The flashes of bluish light from the TV reminded him of a laser light show or maybe the Northern Lights. His eyelids drooped, and his mind buzzed with thoughts of just about everything except facts about South American rainforest plants.

Improvements for his smoke bomb designs, new martial arts moves, images of walruses, and walruses performing martial arts bounced around in his mind like thousands of sugar-addled chimps in a cathedral.

And yet ... he just couldn't keep his eyes open.

* * *

Thorium pressed a button with his left hand. The screen flashed, and the Portobellos' living room was enveloped in a green glow that emanated from the television.

The form lying on the couch was still in the shape of a thirteen-year-old boy, but Dr. Thorium and Floofles could now see through Alex's skin and observe his skeletal and muscle structure. And his brain. A brain that throbbed and pulsated like a giant heart. Tiny bolts of electricity arced from one side of the boy's brain to the other.

"This is it," Thorium whispered, licking his lips as he continued to ease the lever downward.

* * *

"During the summer, most Pacific walruses can be found north of the Bering Strait in the Chukchi Sea. Walruses occupy beaches in large numbers, where they gather together for warmth and companionship."

Just before his eyes closed, Alex thought he saw the light coming from the TV change from blue to a neon green, but it must have been his imagination.

As he dozed off, images of night vision goggles, utility belts with pouches stuffed with grappling hooks and boomerangs, flashy capes and cowls, and Emperor Qin Shi Huang flashed through his mind almost too quickly to comprehend.

And in the middle of it all was an island, a land mass in the Chukchi Sea somewhere near the Bering Strait. It was as if Alex were viewing the island from a descending airplane, giving him a bird's-eye view that drew closer to the island by the moment.

It was a plain, dark gray, rocky island surrounded by floating chunks of ice. As the island came into focus, Alex saw a herd of walruses, about two hundred, each standing on its rear flippers and thrusting its front flippers forward methodically. They were practicing some sort of martial art—his martial art.

Like a school of Shaolin monks, the blubbery sea mammals punched and kicked and bellowed in unison. Their folds of flabby skin flapped and undulated like bowls of gelatin during an earthquake.

Each walrus threw a fearsome punch with its left flipper and turned its head, looking at Alex with its deep, soulful, black eyes.

They were beckoning him.

* * *

Dr. Thorium could see tiny sparks popping off the boy's pulsating brain, his neurons pushed far beyond what most human cerebrums could handle. The boy remained motionless.

Little balls of sweat dripped down Thorium's face as he glanced from the viewscreen to his right hand grasping the lever and back to the viewscreen. The energy core was almost at its full capacity.

He held his breath and yanked the lever all the way down. Alex's brain glowed a bright green and sparked like a firework about to blow. Just for a second, Dr. Thorium wondered about the ethical implications of exposing a teenager to experimental radiation.

There was a fiery KA-BLAM as a shower of fire burst out of the back of the TV. The video feed hadn't been cut, which meant the camera and the energy core were still intact.

The green glow died down, the sparks flickered out, and Alex's brain, though a little larger than it had been, returned to its normal, pink, gooey state.

And it was still throbbing. The tiny, electrical arcs were still hopping across the wrinkly brain, faster than before. Alex still had conscious brain activity and motor function!

"Success!" the scientist shouted, thrusting his fist into the air. He spun around in his chair and snatched Floofles from the floor, planting a kiss on his growling Chihuahua's lips. "We've done it, Floofles! We've done it! Superhuman intelligence realized!"

Thorium set Floofles on the laboratory floor and spun the chair around again and again. He giggled like a schoolgirl, and a few tears escaped his eyes. Then he turned his attention to the sleeping boy on his viewscreen.

"Get some rest, young Portobello," he murmured. "For tonight, both your life and human intelligence as we know it have marched forward into the unknown!"

Chapter 6

"Good afternoon, class," Ms. Grunderson said from her desk as the bell rang and her students settled into their seats. "Today we'll continue our discussion on rainforests and other ecosystems. But first, Alex, I believe we have some unfinished business."

Alex blew across the top of his desk, scattering eraser shavings. He hadn't had time to finish his essay last night and had tried to finish it before leaving for school this morning, but there were just so many other ideas buzzing around in his mind.

So he'd worked on the essay during the ride to school and had finished it just before Ms. Grunderson called on him.

The chattering of his classmates died down as the other students scooted their chairs closer to their desks. It was so quiet that Alex could hear the swooping of the fan blades rotating above his head.

He straightened his back and marched toward the front of the classroom.

Running his fingers through the stack of papers that contained his rainforest essay, he muttered under his breath about "incompetent educators" and "unappreciated scientific progress" and "using vibrissae to locate sources of food." The poster of the smiling train on the back wall of the classroom seemed to be laughing at him.

Finally, he stood in front of the class. Two dozen pairs of drooping eyes were locked onto him like a gaggle of basset hounds watching educational television. Alex cleared his throat and began to read:

"The Amazon rainforest contains a variety of animal and plant life, including the rubber tree and heliconia flower. The rainforest also contains the cacao plant, from which we get chocolate, and the passion fruit flower, which is used to make passion fruit juice.

"Each of these plants contributes to the tropical, temperate ecosystem of the rainforest in a unique way and—"

Alex stopped.

"In a unique—"

Alex felt a little jolt inside his head, like a tiny, tusk-bearing sea mammal was thumping against his brain, urging him to use his talents, not to hide them under a blubbery layer of shame.

He lowered the hand-written papers, and a smile crept across his lips. "In a unique environment characterized by high temperatures and rain. Heavy showers of rain. Like the rain that pours down on a dark city street, concealing the underhanded dealings and dark deeds that comprise the city's criminal underbelly.

"But with the proper tools ..." Alex raised his index finger and paused for dramatic effect. "With the proper tools, one can combat the crime that clogs the bowels of Cremini City and wage a one-man war on injustice and villainy."

"Alex ...," Ms. Grunderson said, setting her glasses on the desk and pressing her fingers to her forehead.

"Despite the discordant opinions of certain parties—" Alex narrowed his eyes and shot a disapproving glance at Ms. Grunderson. "—

building a crime-fighting arsenal is entirely possible with the proper tools and training."

Snatching a piece of chalk, Alex began to reproduce some of his designs on the chalk board. Bits of chalk flew in every direction as mathematical equations, gadget schematics, vibrissae, and stick figures punching and kicking each other filled the board in a matter of seconds.

Ms. Grunderson stood. "Alex, you can't draw pictures of fighting in class—"

"An advanced knowledge of chemistry and mechanics could theoretically allow one to construct the kind of non-lethal weaponry and tools necessary to disarm and derail the criminal element.

"After all, devices like grappling hooks and smoke bombs already exist. And creating some sort of high-tensile, strength-restraining fluid, similar to comic book web fluid, is just simple chemistry. You could even make it explosive if you wanted.

"Additionally, a device capable of intercepting communication signals could theoretically alert one to crimes in progress by allowing one to listen in on both police communications and the cell phones and radios of criminals themselves.

"Unique martial arts, composed using a superior knowledge of human anatomy, could confuse the criminal element, making it a simple matter of taking one's opponents by surprise in order to—"

"Alex, that's enough. You're not going to use my classroom as an opportunity for—"

"Oh, I'm far from done, Ms. Grunderson."

Alex turned his back to the blackboard to face his classmates. "A brief psychological evaluation of Ms. Grunderson provides many clues as to why she initially rejected the premise of my devices and martial arts designs. Using her numerous, essay-length posts on the school message boards, I've devised my own theory regarding Ms. Grunderson's unlively temperament.

"Due to her less-than-social personality traits, her intermittent incontinence, and her complex and interdependent relationship with her cat, Squiggly, Ms. Grunderson is unable to objectively evaluate ideas that fall outside her strict paradigm."

"Why, you little—!" Ms. Grunderson stomped toward her student.

"Additionally, Ms. Grunderson's near-obsessive love of *The Young and the Restless* gives us a glimpse into her many repressed emotions."

"That's enough, Alex Portobello!"

"But I was just getting to your questionable activities in Cancun in the summer of '74."

Ms. Grunderson's face was as red as a cardinal in a ketchup bath. "Take your seat, Alex," she finally demanded in a deep, warbling voice, closing her eyes and pointing toward Alex's desk. "Your parents will be getting a call from Principal Possumsniffer and me this afternoon."

Chapter 7

Gwen Portobello stood in the corner of her kitchen with the phone clamped to her ear, twirling a lock of her hair as she listened to an exasperated Ms. Grunderson describe Alex's latest antics.

The mid-afternoon sun lit up the turquoise kitchen. The kitchen always felt a little warm in the afternoons, especially after Gwen received troubling news from Alex's school, which she imagined, she received a lot more often than did the mothers of Alex's classmates. She just couldn't see any of the other kids building a lunchmeat-powered, papier mâché dune buggy during history class.

"Uh-huh," Gwen droned into the phone, "Yes, Ms. Grunderson. No, we weren't aware he was putting those things in his presentation. But if

you posted that information online, then—
Really? Intermittently? How does that work?"

Gwen pressed a finger to her forehead as
Alex's teacher continued. "Okay. We'll be having
a talk with him tonight, and we'll tell him to
expect detention and to write an apology letter.
Okay. Yes. Thank you."

Gwen hung up the phone and threw her head
back, rolling her eyes. "That was Alex's teacher,"
she said, plopping into a chair at the kitchen
table across from her husband and Mrs.
Crumpleston, the Portobellos' neighbor.

"Apparently," Gwen continued as she pawed
at the plate of freshly prepared chicken salad
sandwiches on the table, "he psycho-analyzed
her and shared his findings with the class."

Walt Portobello folded his newspaper and set
it on the table next to his coffee. Blowing on his
coffee, he took a sip. "Well, what can we do?
Ground him?"

Gwen shook her head. "And leave him alone
in his room with his inventions for multiple
nights in a row? Doesn't sound like much of a
punishment." She took a small bite of one of the
sandwiches.

"The school is willing to settle for a few weeks detention. Alex's little escapades don't compare to some of the bullying and crime problems Cremini City schools have to worry about, and I get the sense they don't want to push us into switching schools. Alex's GPA really helps them with funding.

"But I don't care how good his grades are; Alex can't go through middle school scoffing at his assignments, insulting his teachers, and talking about crime-fighting gadgets."

"Oh, I don't know about that, dear," said Mrs. Crumpleston as she curled both her hands around her mug of tea and lifted it slowly to her wrinkled lips, dribbling a bit on her sweater, "My grandson Norbert went through a rebellious phase when he was living with Harry and me."

She took another sip of tea. "He purchased about seventeen Rottweilers and tried to teach them to waltz. The dogs didn't take to it, and long story short, I can't so much as smell a dog these days without going into a fit of hysterics."

Mrs. Crumpleston's eye twitched a little. "But Norbert eventually turned his life around. You know, after the stitches and the surgeries and the decades of therapy."

Walt cleared his throat. "Well, there's just one thing left to do: we'll have to consider this his second strike."

"His what?" Gwen asked.

"His second strike. You remember, don't you? Three weeks ago, after he dunked the Hendersons' rabbits in Nair to make them more aerodynamic? We told him that was his first strike. And three strikes means …."

"Three strikes means he goes to Colonel Primpington's Boarding School." Gwen straightened her mouth. "I don't want to have to send him there, Walt. Every time we mention it, all the color drains from his face."

"We'll just have to hope it doesn't come to that. And if it does …." Walt stretched his hands across the table, gripping his wife's fingers. "It'll be fine. You'll see. Alex'll grow into an upstanding, productive member of society before you know it."

* * *

"Just a little more plutonium phosphate …."

Alex's fingers quivered as he tipped the test tube ever so slightly toward the beaker of bubbling, green chemicals. It sat on a Bunsen burner next to the eyedropper full of partially de-weaponized uranium.

He'd placed the uranium across from the miniature tesla coils and the series of tubes that twisted and turned and twined around each other like a roller-coaster of glorious science.

The bedroom was even more crowded now than it had been a few days ago. Alex had moved most of his experiments and devices from the living room to his bedroom. For some reason, ever since he'd left for school that morning, the living room TV had made Alex uneasy.

A series of empty cardboard boxes and chemical tanks were piled in the corner near the head of the bed. He'd recently been able to purchase some of the more ... interesting ... chemical compounds from Questionable Science, Incorporated.

Their night janitor, as Alex had recently learned, accepted valuable comic books and rare variants of half-chewed gum as payment.

Alex used a wooden slab that slid out from the right side of the computer desk as a chemistry table. Earlier this afternoon, he'd thrust the wooden slab out from the main part of the desk with such force that he'd put a small hole in the wall. But he couldn't help it. His whole body quivered with anticipation like the stomach of a fat man starring in *Riverdance.*

Just a few drops of the yellow liquid were enough. Alex giggled and leaned forward, locking his eyes on the bubbling, purple concoction that glowed so brightly it lit the whole bedroom. The sweet smell of chemicals was almost overpowering but, Alex thought, that's just the price one pays for scientific discovery.

"Provided it hardens properly, this chemical will serve as the perfect base for my 'blubber' crime-fighting compound. Now, let's see that everything else is in order."

Alex tiptoed around the slab of chemicals and glassware and the computer desk and slid to his bed, where a tan, rounded piece of hard rubber sat. Tiny white fibers covered the surface of the rubber, all angled downward like fur on a cat. At the top of the piece of rubber were two small, oval-shaped holes.

Lifting the top off his new device, Alex examined the inside. Each fiber was interconnected in a mesh of other wires and circuit boards, all soldered together. He squinted and nodded.

"Yes, I'd say the communications interceptors are properly arrayed. And the grappling hook guns and smoke bombs and mask lenses won't take long to prepare."

Reaching behind his bed, Alex felt around, past the pile of half-eaten pickled herring sandwiches, and pulled out a thin cardboard color wheel.

"I suppose all that's left to do is choose a color scheme."

Chapter 8

The snick-snick-snick of the sewing machine stopped at last. It was dark outside, and the computer desk and other furniture cast long shadows across the bedroom. The window was closed, making the room warm and a little stuffy.

Not a sound entered or exited. It was quiet as a toothless woman at a steak auction.

At last, Alex was finished. He laid the completed costume on his bed and nodded. Perfect. It'd taken more than a few trips to Bicyclist World to find just the right kind of spandex, and he'd spent the whole afternoon cutting apart and stitching together different sections of a few dozen pairs of royal blue cycling shorts.

But the body suit was perfect, just tight enough to give him the full range of movement while leaving the exact shape of his buttocks to the imagination.

He took off his clothes, slipped into the suit, and draped the cape over his shoulders. The mask portion of the cowl hung behind his neck.

He snatched the communications interceptor from the desk and ran his fingers through the tiny antennae bristled like whiskers all over the soft, brown plastic shell. Two long white fang-shaped pieces now jutted from the bottom of the device.

Alex clipped the interceptor in place on his chest, just below his neck, and hooked both sides of his jet-black cape into the straps behind it to keep the cape in place. He pulled on the gloves and boots, then looked out the window at the streets below.

Taking a step back from the window, he blinked a few times, shaking his head. "What am I thinking?" Alex said to no one in particular. He began to pace around the room, his cape rippling over the spare mechanical parts that littered the floor.

At last, his eyes settled on the inflatable, pop star-shaped punching bag. He stopped in front of the effigy of Spanky St. Jivestrunky and spoke to it like he was talking to a friend.

"Now that I'm actually in the uniform, this whole thing does seem a little ridiculous. The suit, the cape, the cowl, the gadgets…if Mom or Dad or Ms. Grunderson or someone else finds out about this, they'll think I've lost not one, but all of the marbles in my possession."

The inflatable punching bag didn't answer.

"But if I go out on patrol tonight and Mom and Dad find out, that'll be strike three for sure: a one-way trip to Colonel Primpington's."

St. Jivestrunky continued to stare at him wordlessly. Alex sighed.

"I guess I should at least try on the mask and utility belt."

He flipped the cowl over his head. A shiver, like the one he'd felt that fateful day he'd tried dipping his toes in warm Dijon mustard, crept up his spine as he peered through the eyeholes for the first time. The cowl's corrective lenses made the whole room clearer. It was just like looking through his glasses.

Alex strode back to the window and pushed it open, feeling the crisp night breeze as he clipped the golden utility belt around his waist. There wasn't much activity on his suburban street, but he heard the usual sirens and shouting just a few blocks over.

This time of night always reminded Alex that the criminal element infested downtown Cremini City like '70s Jazzercize DVDs infested his Aunt Gertrude's living room.

He frowned. Each of those echoing screams came from an innocent citizen.

The doubts fell from Alex's mind. "The time for preparation is over." Stepping onto the windowsill with one leg, he fixed his eyes on the city skyline.

"Tonight. Tonight, I show evildoers what it is to feel one's armpit hairs tingle with fear."

* * *

Darkness enveloped downtown Cremini City. The sun had gone down long ago, and the streetlights had flickered on as soon as Cindy Forkinstern left the office. Cindy's shoes clacked against the sidewalk as she hurried to the bus station.

She'd stayed late to finish the budget report. There weren't many people on the road. The walk from work to the bus station wasn't too long, but it was just a little too quiet. And it wound through some of the seedier parts of town.

Cindy heard something ping against the asphalt behind her and increased her pace without looking back. She stared at each streetlight like it was a torch guiding her through a dark cave.

At last, she reached the alley. The clatter of a trash can lid echoed from the dark passageway, and a stray cat shrieked somewhere in the distance. The streetlights and lights above the buildings' back doors didn't illuminate the alley much.

She could see well enough to make out everything between the two buildings, but just barely. The dumpster, the fire escapes, and just about everything else in the alley cast a shadow large enough to hide an elephant.

Cindy took a deep breath. There was no way she'd be able to catch her bus unless she took the shortcut through the alleyway. At last, she started into the alley.

Her eyes darted across the alley, and she started to jog, dashing from light to light. Then she broke into what was almost a run. Despite the chilly night and cold of the shadows, she began to sweat. She clutched her purse and clenched her teeth, focused on the end of the alleyway.

"Evenin', miss," said a slimy voice from behind her.

Cindy stumbled a bit, then whirled around to see a tall man in a long, brown overcoat and a fedora. In his hands he held a plate of birthday cake with a single candle blazing on top.

Half a dozen other figures clad in party hats and colorful streamers emerged from the alley's shadows, each one slowly humming "Happy Birthday to You."

Cindy took a step back. "What do you want?" she cried, her voice cracking.

"The boys and I were just out for an evening stroll," Felix Cumpleaños said, a smirk plastered on his face. "A lovely lady like yourself shouldn't be out this late unescorted. You never know who you're going to run into in this town."

A man in a pointy, purple hat took a step closer to Cindy and produced a party favor bag from his jacket. From the bag, he pulled a kazoo, a noisemaker, and a knife. Another fellow began slowly unwrapping a present. Cindy didn't want to guess what was inside.

The gaggle of partygoers closed in on Cindy as she struggled to back away. "That purse looks heavy, miss," Felix said. "Maybe we could help ... relieve you of it?"

Cindy whipped out her phone and fumbled with the buttons, her eyes popping from the phone to the gangsters and back to the phone. "Hello, police?" she cried, slapping the phone to her ear, "I'm in an alleyway near Siegel and Kirby Street. There's a man menacing me with a cake knife and wearing a—"

The knife-wielding partygoer grabbed his weapon by the blade and flung it. The blade smashed into the side of Cindy's phone, knocking it out of her hand and scattering smart phone pieces all over the asphalt.

Cindy's lip quivered. She continued to step backward and stumbled over a cola can. Her back touched a brick wall. There was nowhere to run.

One of the goons scraped a baseball bat across the front of the dumpster and snickered. Cindy swallowed, and her legs quivered. She slowly reached for her purse, her hands cold. Just then, a clang came from the fire escape on the other side of the alley.

Felix reached into the pocket of his overcoat and gripped something, probably his signature hand-held mini confetti cannon. Everyone in Cremini City knew about the Birthday Gang's weapons, how they fired streamer and confetti blasts deadlier than any gunshot.

"I'm still waiting on that purse, ma'am. I'm a pretty patient man, but my associates can get a bit ... restless at times."

"Interesting. I'm feeling a bit antsy myself," said a booming voice from across the alley.

Felix and his gang whirled around to face the building behind them. Looking down from the fire escape was a stranger dressed in a blue spandex body suit, hands on his hips.

The character wore long, yellow gloves and boots, and a golden utility belt covered in metal compartments lined his waist. The top of the figure's head and face were hidden by a black cowl with lenses in the eye holes, and his cape billowed in the evening breeze like a flag on a windy day.

On his chest was a squishy-looking, tan apparatus covered in tiny whiskers. It had two nostril-like holes at the top and two long, white, horn-shaped pieces jutting out of the bottom.

Cindy wasn't sure if she was imagining things, but she could've sworn the costume's chest piece looked like the nose and mouth of ... a walrus?

"Who the frosting are you?!" Felix demanded, yanking his confetti cannon out of his pocket.

"I am the Crispy Bacon of Vengeance that sizzles in the night," the stranger answered.

Chapter 9

"Waste him!" Felix shouted to his dazed crew, his hand still grasping the confetti cannon. As two of the gang members aimed their party popper pistols across the alley and fired at the hooded man on the fire escape, the strange figure leapt into the air.

The blasts hit the fire escape with a series of pings, scattering sparks and confetti into the night. Reaching into the folds of his cape, the stranger produced a handful of marble-sized, red balls, which he cast onto the ground. The balls hissed. Bursts of heavy smoke flooded the alley.

* * *

Alex grinned as the Birthday Gang cursed and stumbled into each other as they grappled with their weapons. He landed outside the smoky cloud and twisted a knob on the outside of the cowl near his ear. A pair of glowing, green lenses flipped down over the mask's normal lenses. Through the smoke, he could now see the heat signatures of each member of the gang, their arms flailing like they were siamang gibbons in a break-dancing contest.

The spandex-clad lad jumped into the cloud and struck one of the thugs on the jaw. The cake-wielding fiend dropped as another hoodlum stumbled in from the left, raising a blackjack above his head. Alex kicked to his left, catching the festive criminal in the gut.

Alex hopped into a defensive position, his fists at the ready, and heard a bang from outside the smoke cloud. A man with a party blower in his mouth stood next to the alley's dumpster, smacking his baseball bat against it.

"I don't know what your game is, you little party pooper," he snarled, "but I'll teach you to respect the Birthday Gang, just like all the other peons in this city."

Running his fingers along the utility belt, Alex flipped open one of the compartments. He produced a capsule about the size of his thumb and flung it.

The capsule hit the wall above the villain and burst, coating a section of the brick wall about the size of a capybara in a thick, beige goo.

"What the icing is that supposed to be?" the devious partier shouted. He smacked his bat against the dumpster again.

Alex strode toward the ruffian as the smog dissipated. "It's a viscous compound of my own design that expands on contact with oxygen," he explained, "I call it 'blubber.' It's adhesive, extremely strong ..."

Alex reached into his utility belt, pulled out a detonator, and pressed the button. "... and explosive."

The section of wall above the bat-wielding bad guy blasted apart, raining bricks on the stunned gangster and knocking him unconscious.

The blubber worked! Alex wanted to squeal with delight, like a chimp putting on a fresh-from-the-dryer pair of tighty-whities. But that'd blow the whole "dark, mysterious hero" mystique he was going for. Still, he couldn't help but grin.

He dashed to the other side of the alley, punching out one of the hoodlums as he neared their fedora-clad leader. Felix Cumpleaños had run as soon as Alex had hit the ground, and he now stood near the innocent woman at the other end of the alley.

The woman was about sixty feet away from Alex. She hadn't dared move. Four other Birthday Gang toughs were crowded between the end of the alley and the street, cutting off her escape route.

"What do we do, Felix?!" one of the mobsters shouted. Sweat stained his purple party hat.

"Uh … shoot him, you morons!" the gang leader yelled. "Don't let him get any closer!"

Popper pistol blasts and streamers flew toward Alex, but his hours playing "Dance, Dance Junta" on expert mode to build up his agility paid off as he hopped from one side of the alley to another, making himself impossible to hit.

He grabbed one of the grapple guns attached to the side of his utility belt and aimed at the far end of one of the fire escapes, just above the fedora-wearing fiend and his would-be victim.

A golden hook attached to a long cord shot from the gun like a piece of spaghetti out of a laughing woman's nose, wrapped itself around the railing, and yanked Alex forward. He soared across the alley, landing a kick on the back of one of the evil partygoer's heads as he flew by.

"He's getting closer, Felix," Cumpleaños' minion groaned.

A strange specter of spandex, Alex landed about two strides from the gang leader. Felix's eyes darted around the alley. Raising his confetti cannon, he aimed it straight at the innocent woman. She gasped and then froze, putting her hands up as she stared down the barrel of the colorful, deadly party favor.

"All right, Walrus Boy!" Felix shouted, "One step closer, and the chick gets it!"

Alex froze. He felt the blood drain from his face as he stared at the woman locked in fear. He dropped the grapple gun and raised his arms, showing the crime boss his empty hands. He swallowed.

The woman glanced at Alex; her eyes popped to Alex's left and back again. *She's frightened*, Alex thought at first. But then she made the same eye motion a second time. Alex raised an eyebrow.

He glanced to his left and spotted a small, less lethal-looking party popper hanging on the belt of one of the gangsters who was lying unconscious about a foot away. At the speed of thought, Alex shot to the gangster's side, snatched the popper, aimed, pulled the string, and fired.

Before Felix could react, a colorful ball of sparks lit up his wrist. Felix snapped his hand upward and fired his confetti cannon into the air, screaming, "Pin my donkey tail, that hurt!"

The men at the end of the alley took off running, leaving Felix alone with the blubbery avenger. Before Cumpleaños could regain his composure, Alex struck the festive hooligan between the eyes. Felix collapsed.

Alex exhaled and relaxed his knees. Now that all his enemies were immobilized or unconscious, he realized how sore his muscles were. And he was sweating profusely. The suit looked cool, but it didn't allow for much ventilation, so now it stuck to his body. And not in a good, cover-one's-toes-in-organic-spray-cheese-and-wax-paper-for-fun kind of way.

Straightening his back, Alex strode to the woman. Her legs had given out, and she'd fallen to the ground. Her eyes were still wide.

"Are you all right, uh ... citizen?" he asked, extending his hand.

"Yes," she said. She gripped his gloved hand and stood up, brushing the dirt off her dress. She took a deep breath and looked at her rescuer. "You just saved my life!"

"No thanks are necessary. When I see an innocent in danger, I'm like a mischievous child with a shaving razor staring at a long-haired camel: action is inevitable!"

The lady giggled, and the color returned to her face. "You're a little short to be punching out criminals, aren't you? And shouldn't a gallant hero put on deodorant before he goes into battle?"

"Justice has neither a height nor a stench, ma'am."

Now that the Birthday Gang goons were either knocked out or gone, the alley was quiet once again. But the faint sound of sirens grew closer. It wasn't long before Alex heard car doors slamming.

He retracted the grappling hook cable into his pistol and snapped the hook back in place.

"I have to go now," he said, peering at the rooftop of one of the buildings. "Next time, might

I suggest you travel down a less treacherous alley?"

"Wait!" the woman shouted as Alex shot his grapple gun and hooked the ledge of a neighboring building's roof. "Your name. At least tell me who you are."

Alex turned, his cape still flapping in the night breeze. "I am the Black Walrus. And I am the Cheeto dust that stains the fingers of injustice."

Activating the grapple gun's retractor, Alex zipped into the air and out of sight.

Chapter 10

"This is Max Blatherson for Channel 38 News, reporting from the intersection of Siegel and Kirby Streets. Some mysterious goings-on in the city streets tonight: almost every member of the notorious Birthday Gang, which has eluded the police for years, was found unconscious in an alleyway, as if waiting for Cremini City's finest to put them behind bars.

"I'm here with Cindy Forkinstern, who claims a young vigilante rescued her from the gang before disappearing."

Gwen Portobello stepped into the living room and stood behind her husband, who was seated on the couch watching the news.

Static clouded the image, and the news report blinked on and off and kept flickering different colors; Gwen could barely tell what was going on. Every few seconds, she heard a loud pop from the television.

"What's wrong with the TV?" she asked.

"I'm not sure," Walt responded, putting his fingers to his chin. "It's been doing this all night, and there are a few singe marks on the carpet behind it. I'll pick up a new TV tomorrow. I know I should turn it off, but when I heard about what happened downtown, I couldn't just ignore the news report."

Even through the static-covered broadcast, Gwen could make out the bruises on the Birthday Gang members as officers hauled them into police cars. She put her hand to her mouth and bit her thumb nail as she listened to Max Blatherson's report.

"Vigilantism? Isn't there enough shady stuff going on in this city? We're trying to raise a child here, Walt."

Walt shifted his leg to the top of the other knee. "I don't think that gang would've responded to a firm talking-to, hon. Could be just what this city needs."

Gwen sighed through her nose. "Where's Alex? He'd be interested in this."

"He said he was going to go 'perch on the roof and brood.' You know how kids are these days."

* * *

The darkness hid Alex beneath his billowing black cape. He could still hear police sirens blaring downtown. The house had a roof that slanted just-so, allowing Alex to crouch like a gargoyle and glare at the city skyline outside his neighborhood.

"I have seen the darkness that poisons this city," he said to no one in particular. "Darkness that eats away at its blooming onion-like soul. Darkness that requires an angsty, inner monologue."

The night breeze made the trees quake a little.

"The Birthday Gang is just the beginning. Based on what I've picked up on the communications interceptors, the threats to Cremini City are vast.

"I know not how many avocados and beans reside in the seven-layer dip of villainy. But this I do know: as long as blood flows through the blubbery veins of the Black Walrus, evil will have no place to hide."

* * *

Ravenously, Floofles gobbled down his evening bowl of dog food in the kitchen of Dr. Thorium's facility. The tiny Chihuahua swallowed the last mouthful of dry kibble and exhaled through his tiny nostrils.

He missed the Gigantocorp office, the one with all the nice businessmen in their fancy suits and ties. There, Floofles could get away from Dr. Thorium's lab and lay on the leather office couch in a sunbeam while old-school jazz played on the radio.

And sometimes the businessmen would leave their sandwiches a little too close to the edge of the lunchroom table, allowing Floofles to slink his way to the table, hop up, and snag a cold cut or two.

The small break room at his master's new facility contained Floofles' food bowl and bed, a fridge, a microwave, and a sink, and it was separated from the rest of the lab by a thick, metal door. The kitchen was the only place Floofles could find peace from his master's experiments and his ... eccentric personality.

Behind the metal door that led to the lab came the usual series of sparks, snaps, explosions, and cries of frustration. Through the rectangular window on the lab door, the Chihuahua saw a series of green flames flying from Thorium's workstation.

"No. No, that's not right, either. It's not right! Curses!"

The smash of glass echoed throughout the facility. Floofles rolled his little eyes. His master was in one of his moods again.

The door flew open. Dr. Thorium trudged out, massaging his forehead, his gloved hands covered in burn marks.

His normally pristine lab coat was full of holes, the red "TL" logo was frayed, and his hair was matted and greasy from days without showering. He slammed his fists on the kitchen counter and turned to his Chihuahua.

"Why must my toil be in vain, Floofles?!" the singed scientist cried, dropping to his knees in front of the little dog. "I've tried every configuration, every power source, and I just can't recreate the tissue-altering power of the energy core."

Dr. Thorium snatched Floofles from the floor and held him at eye level. "It's just a budget issue. That's all. Back when I was working for

Gigantocorp, I had all the money in the world to finance my experiments."

He stood, holding Floofles in the crook of his arm and putting his wrist to his forehead. "But ever since they fired me, I've had to subsist off the profits from selling my series of workout videos and homemade panda jerky. It's just not enough to afford the isotopes needed to recreate the core."

Thorium held the growling Chihuahua to his chest as he paused, thinking. Finally, he bowed his head and let out a sigh as he carried Floofles into the lab.

The walls were covered in singe marks, and a huge hole had been burned in the center of one of the chemical tables. Most of the floor robots were overturned, their internal circuits blown halfway across the lab. The robotic arms on a few of them still twitched and sparked.

Setting Floofles on the floor, Dr. Thorium trudged to his closet. *The* closet. The one he'd sworn he'd never open again after the incident at the electronics store. He hefted a dusty trunk from the closet and set it on the lab floor with a thunk.

Flipping open the trunk's lid, Dr. Thorium produced a set of black gloves, lock-picking tools, and a ray gun.

"I never thought I'd say this, Floofles my friend," he said, stretching the gloves over his fingers, "but we have no option. Our camera was fried a few minutes after the energy core blew a hole in the Portobellos' TV, so we no longer have any visual on the house's interior.

"But the good news is that the core should still be intact. We must retrieve it from the Portobello household. By any means necessary."

Chapter 11

The school buzzed with excitement as Alex strutted down the halls. All day long, he'd been listening to rumors fly back and forth among his classmates.

"Did you hear about that Black Walrus guy? The one from last night? I heard he took out the whole Birthday Gang single-handedly!"

"I heard he has a belt full of explosives and gadgets and stuff."

"Walrus-Fu. That's what we're calling his martial art. My uncle's a cop, and he told me the Birthday Gang said the Walrus took them out with a totally unique fighting style."

"Dude, I heard the Black Walrus' tusks can detect the evil in the human soul."

"And if you've been good all year, the Black Walrus comes down your chimney early Labor

Day morning and leaves you a two-liter bottle of orange soda and an assortment of fine cheeses."

For once, the echoes of chattering didn't seem distracting or annoying. On his way to math class, Alex passed by the "Go Cremini City Middle School Fighting Proboscis Monkeys!" poster. But this time, next to it was a Black Walrus Fan Club sign-up sheet.

Some kids said the Black Walrus wasn't a human at all but was actually a vengeful Inuit spirit come to Earth to cleanse the world of evil (Alex liked that rumor.)

Others said the Black Walrus was just a dejected fast-food worker who got bored with his day job, put on long underwear, and started beating up criminals as an indirect way to audition for the Cremini City Ballet (Alex didn't like that rumor.)

Drew Patterson thought the Black Walrus was just a concept that lives inside of everyone, kind of like the Spirit of Christmas. Only instead of encouraging everyone to give of themselves and help those in need, the Black Walrus, with his shiny tusks and spandex, was there to remind us of the importance of dental hygiene and tightly-fitting bicycle shorts (Alex wasn't sure how to feel about that one.)

The bell rang, and Alex walked down the hallway, heading home for a well-deserved, oily shin massage from Fabrizio, one of his trained guinea pigs. Like they had a few days before, the sounds and smells of the middle school faded from his mind as Alex began to daydream about the Black Walrus' next escapade.

Maybe he'd tackle a gang of international drug smugglers dressed as platypuses or a real, honest-to-pork-rinds villainous mastermind! After all, who knows what evil lurks in the hearts of—

Alex lurched to a stop as the smell of chewing gum struck him. He'd been so lost in his own mind, he'd almost bumped into Tracy.

"Hi, Alex," she snapped through her gum, "Did you hear about all this Black Walrus stuff? Pretty crazy, huh?"

Alex took off his glasses and rubbed the lenses with his shirt. "An ordinary citizen who chooses to protect innocent citizenry by taking justice into his own hands? No, I don't think that's crazy at all."

Tracy stepped to Alex's side so they could walk to the front door together. "Are you serious? Alex, someone like that might get hurt or killed. And I'm pretty sure being a vigilante is against the law."

She grinned coyly. "If I didn't know better, I'd think you were connected to the Black Walrus somehow."

Alex flicked his wrist like he was throwing away a wheel of rotten weasel cheese. "Hogwash. Like most of the other students, I'm just easily stimulated by stories of heroism and find the idea mysterious and intriguing. It's healthy, you know. Keeps us off the streets and away from those back-alley chinchilla-tossing competitions."

"Oh." Tracy cleared her throat. "So ... what are you doing after school today?"

"Managing my online auctions. That and working on some ... personal projects. I've been looking for a large, empty, out-of-the-way space I can use for a ... yoga studio ... and there's a place I have in mind."

The bright sunlight hit them both as Tracy and Alex walked outside. "By yourself again? Why don't you come over to my house or come to the fan club meeting or something? Everyone likes being alone sometimes, but a lot of us are starting to wonder whether you live somewhere inside the school and just come out to go to class."

"Hmm," Alex mumbled. Tracy had a good point. He'd been spending so much time preparing for his activities as the Black Walrus, he hadn't given much thought to maintaining a secret identity in order to protect his parents and friends from evildoers or media exposure.

The horde of coffee-drinking meerkats that was Alex's brain was forming a conga line of inspiration again. If he scouted out the location he had in mind in secret, on his own, someone might get suspicious. But if he brought someone else ....

Before she could finish her thought about history class or gum or whatever she was talking about, Alex spotted Tracy's mom's car and pointed it out to her. He sprinted home and threw open the door to the kitchen, panting.

"3:32? You're home early." Alex's mom stopped chopping carrots and set her knife down on the cutting board. "What's going on, sweetie?"

Alex bent over and placed his hands on his knees. "Oh nothing, Mom," he said between gulps of air. "Just enjoying the beautiful afternoon sunshine after spending another enthralling day in our superb education system."

"Okay ...." Mom wiped her hands on her purple sweater, folded her arms, and leaned back against the stove, eyeing her son.

"I was just thinking," Alex said, regaining his composure. "When was the last time we went to the zoo?"

"The zoo? We haven't been to the zoo since you were eleven. They kicked us out after you handed out rubber band guns to all the sloths, remember?"

"Oh, that's right." Alex shuddered as he thought back to the sinister-looking sloths and the blitzkrieg of rubber bands raining down on the zoo employees as they dove for cover. He sat down and drummed his fingers on the kitchen table. "Do you think they remember that?"

"Probably. I still have the stack of letters we got from the zoo officials, including the one from that Brinkles lady from the Pinniped Department that smelled like pickle brine and called you a 'rotten little gherkin.'

"But we can always see if they'll let bygones be bygones. Thursday's a school holiday. Would you like to go to the zoo then?"

"Yes, please."

Mom narrowed her eyes. "Why?"

"Uh ... I want to apologize to the sloths and make sure the employees' welts have healed. And I want to get some new photos of koala rear ends for my bedroom wall. They're such fascinating creatures."

"Okay." Alex's mom pressed one of her fingers to her forehead. Alex wasn't sure whether she believed him about the sloths and koalas, but she clearly wasn't in an argumentative mood. She picked up her knife and began chopping carrots again.

"Your father set the old TV out with the trash. I still have no idea what happened to it. You remember your father and I are going to the Porkstons' house to play bridge tonight, don't you?" Mom changed the subject as she increased the speed of her chopping. "You sure you'll be okay by yourself?"

"Yes," Alex said.

Mom slapped the knife down on the cutting board and turned to Alex, putting her hands on her hips. "Are you sure?"

"Don't worry about me, Mom. You and Dad go out and have a nice time. I'll just ... keep watch."

Chapter 12

Alex cracked open another can of carbonated chipmunk milk and chugged it as fast as he could. The sun was setting, and the pinkish-purple light of the evening seeped into the window. It was a little hot and stuffy in the bedroom; he'd had the door closed for the last few hours.

Grumbling to himself, Alex shifted in his computer chair and clicked through the same series of windows on his laptop, checking once again on his KneeBay auctions.

The auctions were all listed under the name Odobenus Lover, a fake name Alex could use to further hide his identity. Someone had made an offer on the gravity-defying toe socks, and a bidding war was already underway for the self-regenerating tofu. Infinite tofu had serious potential.

Alex sighed. He didn't like selling his old inventions, but if he was going to handle bigger threats to Cremini City, he'd need more equipment. Smoke bombs and grappling hooks would only confuse the criminal element for so long.

Scrolling further down the page, he looked at the "buyer" section and found that he had enough money in the Odobenus Lover account to cover the cost of the new computer components and the parts for the retinal scanner.

But he still had a major problem: shipping. Alex couldn't exactly have the parts for his crime-fighting gadgets shipped to the house without making his parents suspicious and increasing his likelihood of being shipped to Colonel Primpington's. He needed to find a new base of operations soon.

Alex minimized the auction window and glanced once again at the security camera footage. He'd told his parents he was going to keep watch over the house and didn't intend to break his word. Alex was even wearing his Black Walrus suit beneath his clothes just in case something nefarious went down.

He switched from the front yard security camera (the trash was by the curb awaiting pickup, just like it'd been for the last seven hours) to the backyard security camera to the side yard security camera and back again, then leaned back in his chair. Nothing on the cameras.

Wiping the milk mustache off his lips, Alex tossed the milk can onto the floor with all the other cans he'd drained tonight. His stomach burbled. Too many carbonated drinks.

Through the computer speakers, Alex heard the sound of a vehicle ambling down the street. He jumped and switched to the front yard camera. A large, black van crept along the side of the road and pulled up in front of his house.

The van door opened, and a man in a long, white lab coat and goggles hopped out, followed by a Chihuahua. Leaning forward, Alex squinted at the screen.

Maybe the Crumplestons were having a guest over? No, that couldn't be it. Mrs. Crumpleston was terrified of dogs. Were city workers here to repair a power line or something? No. Alex had checked the power distribution system a few weeks ago via his "how many volts can you run through a stalk of celery before it explodes and catches the drapes on fire?" experiment.

The man in the lab coat motioned to the Chihuahua. They began walking up Alex's driveway! The lab-coat-clad man (a scientist, possibly?) stopped and looked to his left.

A smile crawled across his face as he stared at the pile of trash next to the curb. His eyes were locked onto the old TV, which Alex's dad had thrown away that morning.

Alex had a feeling this well-dressed scientist was interested in more than cheap, outdated electronics. The man didn't exactly look like a roughneck criminal type, but the vibrissae of Alex's brain sensed danger.

He'd clearly intended to break into the house and steal the television. Finding the TV at the curb had been a stroke of luck.

Alex knew there was something wrong with that TV! After all, that piece of eerie electronics was the sole reason he'd never worn his Black Walrus garb anywhere in the house but his bedroom, even when he was home alone. Based on the theft in progress, Alex knew his instincts had been on-point.

If Alex let this stranger get away now, he might learn something about Alex's secret identity. Or maybe he'd try to break into the house later to steal something else. Alex's identity, his home, and his parents were in peril.

The chair squeaked across the wooden, bedroom floor as Alex pushed away from his computer desk and stood. He nudged his glasses up on his nose. The time to sit on one's tush in front of the computer screen was over.

Even though he knew he was home alone, Alex instinctively looked over his shoulder before he pulled off his shirt and pants, revealing the blue body suit, gold utility belt, and black cape. Plunging his hands beneath his mattress, he whipped out his yellow boots and gloves.

Alex frowned as he pulled on the boots. Hiding his crime-fighting uniform under the mattress was no way to store garments that were supposed to strike pants-wetting fear into the heart of the criminal underworld. He'd have to look into a better storage system later.

Quiet as a sentient hot dog in a room full of sleeping bull terriers, Alex slid the window open. He tiptoed onto the roof. The evening sky glowed orange, and the neighborhood's trees cast long shadows. It was past dinnertime, so the suburban street was empty and quiet as a nun at a rap concert.

The stranger and his Chihuahua slunk toward the TV. Alex prepared to jump from the roof and onto the TV, but stopped himself, lurching and almost tripping over the cape.

If he jumped down from his own roof, the stranger could connect the Black Walrus to the Portobello house and deduce his true identity. Alex stayed, crouching, on the roof. Better to let the television thief drive a short distance before giving away his position.

The weird man loaded the TV into the back of his van and slammed the back doors shut. He and the Chihuahua hopped back into the vehicle. Alex could hear the strange thief giggling through the van's open driver's side window.

As the car began to move down the road, Alex drew one of his grapple guns from its holster.

The car was picking up speed. He was only going to get one shot.

Alex pulled the trigger, and the grappling hook and cable soared toward the vehicle. As the hook punctured the top of the van, Alex ran down the slope of the house's roof, gaining momentum. He reached the gutter and leaped high into the air as he activated the gun's retractor.

He zipped toward the van and landed on the roof with a thunk. The driver slammed on the brakes, tossing Alex onto the hood. Alex pulled his arms and legs in tight, rolling off the hood and onto the asphalt.

Stumbling to his feet, Alex glared into the eyes of the shocked scientist. "I am the sensitive nose hair that fires the snot of villainy from the nostrils of this city," he said, draping the folds of his cape over his shoulders to look more menacing.

"The Black Walrus … so the rumors are true …," the man behind the wheel trailed off, shifting and slowly extending his arm sideways while making a waving motion with his other hand.

"Well, I'm a reasonable man and certainly no criminal, so I wouldn't dream of standing in the way of the city's new defender. I mean, there's a perfectly reasonable explanation as to why I've just loaded that television in the back of my van, and I'm sure we'll be able to—Floofles, attack!"

Chapter 13

The man behind the wheel popped open the passenger side door and shooed the Chihuahua out. Ignoring its master's command to attack, the Chihuahua wagged its tail as it gazed around the street.

It looked happy to be outdoors. It craned its neck and sniffed toward the Crumplestons' house, the source of the smell of grilling burgers that wafted throughout the neighborhood.

The driver whipped out a laser pistol and blasted through the windshield. The Black Walrus dropped, clinging to the street as the laser beam flew over him. He heard a blast behind him as the beam hit an ice cream truck rolling slowly down the road. As Alex turned his head to view the explosion, he heard an engine revving. The TV thief was trying to escape.

Unbuckling a compartment on his utility belt, the Black Walrus grabbed a handful of blubber pellets and hopped forward, landing on the hood of the van. The vehicle screeched to a stop again. Alex raised his knee, planting his foot on the van's damaged hood.

Vaulting off the hood and into the air, Alex threw the pellets beneath him. The pellets burst, and blubber spewed across the hood. Alex drew the blubber detonator from his belt and pressed the button.

A fiery explosion lit up the engine area of the van, stopping the vehicle for good. Alex landed on the sidewalk across from the driver's side door. Another laser blast rocketed from the van, sending the door flying into Mr. Burpenshire's hedges. The lab-coated stranger hopped from the vehicle.

The stranger held the laser blaster in his left hand, and on his right he wore a purple metallic fist. He looked shaken but was still grinning. This was obviously a man of science who enjoyed showing off his inventions. Alex could relate.

The Black Walrus glanced at the ice cream truck down the street. He breathed a sigh of relief. The laser blast hadn't hit the ice cream man, and he'd been able to climb out of his damaged truck unharmed.

Fire spewed from the front of the ice cream truck, and melted popsicles and liquid Neapolitan oozed out the back, forming a huge puddle. The peddler of frozen goodies slumped onto the sidewalk. He looked as frazzled as that hamster Alex had dropped into a supercollider, but like the hamster, the driver had survived. Alex turned to face the scientist once again.

"I must admit, Black Walrus, I'm impressed," the singed television burglar panted. "I didn't expect anyone to recognize the importance of the device inside that TV. I don't know why you're patrolling this little neighborhood, but since you appear to be an inventor yourself, I'm sure you'll forgive a mere theft. The cause of science demands it."

"You just endangered the life of an innocent civilian," the Black Walrus said, pointing at the ice cream truck driver. "The cause of justice demands you explain what's so important about that TV. Just as the cause of deliciousness demands the consumption of vanilla pudding and minced onion sandwiches."

The stranger sighed. "Well, you can't say I didn't try to reason with you, Walrus. I'll let the city worry about cleaning your charred remains off the asphalt."

The fiend let loose another laser blast. Alex dove to his right to avoid it. He reached into his utility belt, drew out five of the red smoke bombs he'd used against the Birthday Gang in the alley, and tossed them at the stranger. Thick, puce smoke covered the van and the street in front of it.

While its master was distracted, the Chihuahua dashed out from the cloud of smog. The tags on its collar jingled as it made a beeline for the Crumplestons' house. Alex leapt into the fog.

A purple, metal fist smacked into his chin, and the Black Walrus staggered back, rubbing his jaw. The mad scientist emerged from the smoke. He now had a pair of green lenses on his huge, metallic goggles.

"You've got some nice tricks up your sleeve, Walrus. But I think you'll find I've some pretty snazzy gizmos myself."

He extended his metallic fist toward Alex, and a tiny nozzle popped out of the top. A net made of metal cables shot from the nozzle, ensnaring Alex and knocking him to the blacktop.

Alex flailed like an old man trying to swim in a pool full of marmalade. If he hadn't been wearing gloves and boots, the net's cords would've cut into his wrists and ankles.

The scientist chuckled and pointed his steel fist toward the cloud of smoke that surrounded the van. A new nozzle emerged from the fist, and a sharp blast of air blew most of the smoke cloud away.

"Looks like your combat prowess isn't all it's cracked up to be," he laughed. "Just wait until I tell Floofles and those guys on the dejectedscientist.com message board I took down the Black Walrus."

The cocky scoundrel glanced his fist off the van's driver's side door, causing the van to spin around so the back doors faced him and Alex. The scientist tore off the back doors with his metal fist.

There was the TV. Next to it sat a smooth, white device shaped like the top of a large missile. It had some sort of booster on the bottom and backpack-like straps on the front. A jetpack!

"Eeeeeek!"

Alex whirled to his left, still entangled in the net, as a high-pitched, warbly scream pierced the air. Mrs. Crumpleston stood on her front porch, where she'd been grilling hamburgers. She was now backing toward her front door, a look of horror on her face.

Her eyes were locked onto the fuzzy terror before her: a Chihuahua slowly approaching the deck. The tiny dog yipped, and Mrs. Crumpleston leapt like she'd just been bitten by a rabid lemur.

"Help! Someone, please help!" she shouted, holding a spatula in an iron grip and waving it at the Chihuahua like it would ward off the little dog. "I'm afraid of dogs! It's going to eat me! It's going to eat me!"

Wriggling around like a squid on roller skates, Alex began to untangle his arms and legs from the net. Some of the cords slipped off. Alex heard a snap as the scientist clipped on the jetpack's straps, securing himself to the jet booster. He gripped the TV beneath his left arm.

Alex looked down. His legs were almost free. He just had to loosen a few more tangles ....

He looked back toward Mrs. Crumpleston. Sweat streamed down her face as she fumbled for the doorknob and collapsed against the side of her house. Mr. Crumpleston must've been in the den on the other side of the house. He moved pretty slowly and, Alex guessed, hadn't yet been able to reach his wife.

Mrs. Crumpleston kicked against the air as the Chihuahua hopped closer and closer, licking its lips. She kept shouting: "For the love of beef stroganoff, help me!"

A metal extension with a joystick on the end shot out of the jetpack's side, and the wacky man of science gripped it with his steel-coated hand, preparing to take off.

"Well, Black Walrus, I'm afraid I must take my leave," he said. "Not that it hasn't been fun, but I have to return to my lab and prepare to unleash the ultimate good on Cremini City."

Alex heard the jet booster warming up. He looked from the TV thief to the panicked Mrs. Crumpleston and back again. There wasn't time to stop the TV thief and save Mrs. Crumpleston from the terror of the Chihuahua.

His legs finally slipped free. Alex leapt forward, body-slamming the scientist into the side of the van. In the distance, he could hear Mrs. Crumpleston's horrified screams as the Chihuahua licked her defenseless, burger-grease-covered toes.

Alex gritted his teeth. The Chihuahua wouldn't hurt Mrs. Crumpleston, he told himself, and he could help her inside after he'd taken down the scientist.

The net was almost entirely off Alex now. He thrust it off himself and onto the TV pilferer, ensnaring him. In the scuffle, Alex had draped the net over his opponent, but not the jetpack. The booster fired.

With the speed of a jack rabbit wearing track shoes, the Black Walrus jumped back and drew a blubber pellet from his belt. He slammed it onto the ground like a Fourth of July snapper.

Beige blubber fluid splattered all over the net and the asphalt. The jetpack roared skyward and began lifting the lab-coat-wearing stranger into the air, but it stopped about twenty feet off the ground.

The blubber had stuck the bottom of the net to the street, and since the scientist was caught in the net, the jetpack couldn't take off. For a moment, the jetpack strained against the net in a bizarre, airborne tug-of-war. Alex could hear the jetpack's leather straps squeal as they stretched and loosened under the pressure.

With a pop, the jetpack detached from the scientist and soared away. The crook fell to his knees and dropped the TV. Sparks flew from the television as it shattered on the asphalt, sending bits of plastic and screen all over the pavement.

Across the street, Mrs. Crumpleston had gone silent. She lay on her back now, still mouthing soundless screams of terror. She flailed around on the porch while the Chihuahua stood on her stomach, wagging its tail in anticipation of more delicious burger grease. It growled playfully.

A tiny buzzsaw sprang from the scientist's metallic fist and cut through the net in seconds. The net flopped off his shoulders.

The ne'er-do-well took a quick look at the asphalt. He snatched a glowing, green … something (Alex didn't have time to see what it was) and closed his fist around it.

"Your obnoxious gambit is over, villain," the Black Walrus puffed. "I know not what delicious, Cadbury Egg-like secrets that television held, but you'll not be pilfering its treasures this day."

The TV bandit sneered. He raised the metal fist to his face and, careful not to reveal what was inside his other hand, tweaked a knob on the wrist. From across the street, a light flashed on the Chihuahua's collar.

Like a pair of jaws, a metal harness shot from the back of the collar and snapped onto the Chihuahua's body. The harness covered the little dog like a turtle shell with openings for the Chihuahua's head, legs, and tail.

"You've bitten off more than your little tusks can chew, Walrus. The cause of science—"

"Walruses don't use their tusks to chew," Alex interrupted.

"Whatever. The cause of science shall not be denied!"

A miniature jetpack popped from the back of the Chihuahua's harness and rotated to face the scientist. With a yelp, the tiny canine rocketed away from the Crumplestons' porch and flew toward its master. Raising his arm, the strange man grabbed onto the Chihuahua as it flew by. Man and dog soared down the street and into the sky.

Alex reached for his grapple gun, but it was too late. His quarry had escaped like a margarine-coated earthworm through his fingers.

Mrs. Crumpleston had blacked out. The Chihuahua had been too much for her. The ice cream truck driver had gone for help; his destroyed truck still bled butter pecan.

Tossing his cape over his shoulders in as heroic a manner as he could, Alex darted to the Crumplestons' porch and took the old woman's pulse. She was fine, just shaken.

The Crumplestons' front doorknob began to turn. Alex slunk into Mr. Burpenshire's hedges so he could make his way back to his bedroom without being seen.

It may have been the seventeen cans of carbonated chipmunk milk, but Alex had a feeling this wouldn't be his last encounter with the weird TV snatcher and his Chihuahua.

Chapter 14

Floofles shot warm air out of his nose and plopped his head on the side of the dog bed, eyeballing the dry, lifeless kibble in his food bowl. Buzzing and zapping and the occasional explosion reverberated through the tiny kitchen.

The steel door that led to lab was closed tight. Dr. Thorium had been locked in there for hours.

Floofles hated kibble. He knew he was a dog and that dogs were supposed to eat kibble, but he was tired of following Thorium's orders. He couldn't help but think of the sights and smells of the world outside Thorium Laboratories.

Floofles drooled as he daydreamed. Just once, he'd love a chance to be his own dog, to sink his teeth into a nice, juicy steak ... maybe while he listened to that relaxing music they used to play back at Gigantocorp ....

The door to the lab shot open. Black smoke poured from the doorway behind Dr. Thorium, obscuring the lab's interior. The scientist smelled like pork chops ... burnt pork chops ... and portions of his skin were black and charred.

The fresh lab coat he'd put on a few hours ago was full of singe marks and holes, and little fires burned on the tips of his disheveled hairs like tiny candle wicks. Thorium yanked off his fogged goggles, revealing wild eyes.

He fingered a small, glowing device that looked like a green Christmas light. The bottom half of the small, cylinder-shaped energy core was encased in a metal handle that looked like a tiny, wafer-style ice cream cone designed so that Thorium could hold it safely.

The smoke that flooded into the kitchen did nothing to obscure the neon object as it thrummed with power. Thorium held the thing up to Floofles' face, a smile on his lips the size of a watermelon rind.

"I've done it ...," Dr. Thorium stammered in a dry, cracking, squeaky voice. "I've finally done it, Floofles!"

Before Floofles could bark in protest, Thorium grabbed his paws and swung him around and around like they were dancing in a field of daisies. Floofles growled as Thorium pulled him in close and held him under one arm, once again shoving the new device in his face.

"I've improved the energy core, Floofles! Even without a proper budget, I was able to repair the wear and tear the core's suffered over the past few years and make it even better. It's just like it was when we tested it on that Portobello kid, but now it's even more powerful, more compact, and with a few ... special alterations."

The black smoke made Floofles cough. He felt heat radiating from the weird, little machine. Floofles pushed against Dr. Thorium with his paws, trying to get away from the device. He whined and stifled his gag reflex as Dr. Thorium spun around in bliss like a Disney princess in love.

"This improved core has even more potential than the original design; the radiation is almost unstable. The energy contained in this core is so intense, it could power Cleveland for a fortnight. You could launch it into a raincloud and create a downpour that'd make Noah weep with envy.

"Why, I'll bet we could rub it on goats' feet and make them grow wiggly, little toes!" Dr.

Thorium wriggled his fingers as he pawed the device. He seemed to be so enamored with the gizmo that he didn't notice the green sparks flying off it.

"Of course, the effects on human and animal tissue aren't completely known," he continued. Floofles placed his front paws on Thorium's forearm and tried to stand, growling at the quivering, smoking device.

"In its original form, the core bestowed remarkable intelligence on the Portobello boy. I think the core in its improved state could have similar effects. But, like the core itself, the subject of this new radiation might become a little ... unstable ...."

Floofles squirmed and winced. The green sparks had turned into tiny lightning bolts, and the core rattled around inside its metal handle.

"But what's a little mental instability in the name of science? Where would the scientific community be if we didn't take risks?"

The green glow grew brighter and more intense, and a high-pitched whine emanated from the energy core.

"Say hello to the future of Cremini City, Floofles."

In a flash of light, an energy explosion blasted the room, tearing the tile off the kitchen counter with plasma-based fire.

* * *

The sights and sounds and faint manure smell of the Cremini City Zoo enveloped Gwen Portobello as she and her son made their way from one exhibit to another. The zoo hadn't changed much. The alligators lounged on patches of sand, soaking in the sun, and Gwen's convoluted map made the zoo just as hard to navigate as ever.

To her left, penguins dove in and out of pools of water as young children stared in awe through the window into their underwater domain. And to her right, one chimp picked bugs off another while staring at the zoo patrons with an expression that said, "What are you looking at?"

Kids and their mothers shoved past, leaving a trail of peanuts and ice cream cone drips on the cement and asphalt. Gwen squinted to make out the gorilla exhibit. She'd forgotten to bring her sunglasses.

As they drew closer to the enclosure, the smell began to overpower Gwen. She opened her mouth and noticed that the air had a distinct "gorilla" flavor. She glanced behind her to tell Alex, but he was gone—again.

Gwen lowered her eyebrows and sighed. She trudged past the hippos, rhinos, and rare break-dancing tortoises. She knew right where Alex would be: at the walrus enclosure—again.

There he was, sitting on a rock and sticking his thumb in the air like he was an artist taking measurements. He'd found a rock about five feet off the ground under the shade of a tall tree, a perfect observation point, as Alex would say.

Other patrons stared at him and commented to themselves, but of course, Alex didn't notice. He was lost in thought, just like he'd been for most of his life.

The walrus enclosure was a giant pit with chest-high bars around it to keep patrons from falling in. The blubbery, dark-brown sea mammals lounged about on the rock formations just like they'd been doing fifteen minutes ago, occasionally rolling over or slipping into the water.

Alex scribbled in his notebook and muttered to himself, things like "entry tube can go there" and "I wonder if walrus blubber would be enough to insulate a laser cannon from the cold."

"Alex!" Gwen shouted, almost tripping over the "Atlantic Walruses" sign.

Alex jumped and dropped his notebook. "Oh. Hi, Mom. I, uh ... I was just ... observing the walruses again."

"I can see that. Alex, why did you want to spend the whole afternoon here if you were just going to stare at the walrus exhibit? I'm getting a little worried. It's almost like you're hiding something."

Alex cleared his throat and straightened his glasses. "Well, uh ... I am hiding something. I have been for some time. But enough about my 'lederhosen-wearing Gary Coleman clones in the cellar' experiment. I thought you were going to look at the giraffes."

"I thought *we* were going to look at the giraffes." Gwen planted her hands on her hips, trying to ignore the stares of the other zoo visitors as they walked by.

"Alex, what's going on? Your father and I barely see you, and when we do, you act like there's something big you're not telling us."

Alex slid off the rock and dusted rock fragments from his jeans.

"You're right. I'm sorry, Mom. Walruses are just so mesmerizing." Alex glanced longingly back at the walruses just as one crested the water, scattering droplets across the enclosure almost in slow motion.

"The way those walruses use their vibrissae to detect sources of food while underwater ... the way they use their tusks to hoist themselves out of the water like out-of-shape rock climbers ... the way their blubbery bodies ripple when they move like a mainsail in the breeze ... it's almost hypnotic, don't you think?"

Closing her eyes, Gwen pressed her index finger to her forehead. "No Alex, I don't. But can you please just humor your mother for an afternoon and walk around the rest of the zoo with me?"

"Indeed." Alex stuck his index finger in the air and put his other hand on his hip. "To the parakeets!"

Alex plucked his notebook off the ground, shoved it into his Ninjapotamus backpack, and strolled beside his mom toward the bird house, a tall, stucco building that smelled of bird feces and sunscreen.

* * *

Alex watched Mom's eyeline as they entered the bird house so he could determine where she was looking, where her attention was focused.

He felt a little guilty about trying to "ditch" his mom like this, and he certainly didn't want to work his way toward his third strike and Colonel Primpington's, but he was on a mission. He had to sneak away once again. A stealthy, silent sock lost in the dryer he must be.

The sound of the birds' chirping and squawking and screeching grew louder. It reminded Alex of Ms. Grunderson. Countless times, he'd seen his mom lose herself sitting at the kitchen table, watching the robins flit around the front yard.

Alex chuckled to himself. The birds would make a more than adequate distraction.

Once they were inside the bird house, they sat on a nearby bench. Sure enough, as she watched the parakeets and toucans and rufous potoos soar around their enclosure, Mom's eyes glazed over, and her shoulders relaxed.

Alex crept away from his mom's side, out of the bird enclosure, back into the sunlight, and toward a small office building. Actually, it was more of a shack, a standalone building one could easily mistake for a restroom or a very low-budget time machine.

But Alex had done his research on this building's occupant. It was time for a little conference with one of the zoo officials.

Chapter 15

Running his pocketknife along the side of the little, wooden birthday cake, Felix Cumpleaños flicked tiny bits of wood across the cell floor. Whittling wasn't helping to pass the time.

Felix was sitting at the head of the jail cell cot with his feet up. He leaned back against the wall behind him and scanned the cell, looking at the Birthday Gang, all dressed in bright, prison orange, and through the bars at the three guards stationed at the end of the room in front of the metal door that led to freedom. The guards sat at a folding table, playing cards while their cheap radio crackled with the greatest hits of the '80s.

It'd been about a week since the Black Walrus had put them away. None of them had faced his day in court yet, but they were scheduled to be tried in a few days, and the gang's list of offenses was miles long.

Felix was no lawyer, but he guessed that, after their trials, none of the gang would see the outside of a jail cell for a few dozen birthdays at least.

Gary had removed his purple party hat for the first time in months and sat fingering the stringy streamer ball on top of it. Piñata Pete, still wearing his blindfold, flexed his fingers in and out like he was trying to grip something.

The cops had taken his bat away, and he twitched nervously. With nothing to hit, it wouldn't be long before Pete lost it completely. Even Felix's confetti cannon was now in the cops' possession.

Felix kept one eye on the guards to make sure they hadn't noticed his knife. He'd been able to sneak the pocketknife past the cops and into the cell (the incident in the alley wasn't his first encounter with law enforcement, after all.) But the blade wasn't doing him one present-load of good.

The cake he'd whittled did nothing to take his mind off the gang's fate. He raised the sawdust-covered, wooden birthday cake to his face. It sounded silly, but maybe ... maybe if he made a wish ... well, he had nothing better to do. Felix blew across the top of the cake, sending a tiny cloud of sawdust into the air.

With two blasts and a loud crack, the door on the other side of the room slammed to the ground. Someone shot off the hinges! The guards scrambled out of their chairs, fumbling for their pistols, but with another three laser blasts, the figure on the other side of the doorway clipped the cops' holsters, sending their weapons skidding across the cement floor.

The figure sidestepped into the room dragging a garbage bag behind him, his laser tommy gun pointed at the guards. He flicked the weapon's barrel at one of the cop's hips, motioning to the ring of keys on his belt. With one hand in the air, the guard placed the keys on the floor and nudged them with his foot, sliding the keys toward the intruder.

The newcomer cocked his head toward the open doorway, and the cops backed out of the room, hands to the sky. Once he was sure the cops had left, the stranger dropped his garbage bag, hopped onto the table, set down the tommy gun, and produced a cigar case from his silver suit jacket.

Now that the guards were gone, Felix got a good look at the tommy gun. Even though the laser weapon was clearly high-tech, it looked like it was made of wood and steel and had a round drum like something out of a mobster movie. A string of glowing red lights wound around the drum. Without saying a word to Felix and his men, the short figure clipped the end of a red-brown cigar with a picture of a ham on the band and struck a match.

The smoke drifted toward Felix and the gang. It didn't smell like a normal cigar. It smelled like … meat. As the stranger took the first few puffs, he reached over and tweaked the radio dial. The big band sounds of a 1920s swing station filled the room. The stranger removed the cigar … or meat stick … whatever it was … from his mouth, and smoke poured from his nostrils.

"Many happy returns," he said in a high-pitched, squeaky voice. "The coppers won't be back for a few minutes. Just enough time for a few slick operators like yourselves to blow this joint."

He held up the keys to the cell door and jangled them. "Got a proposition for you boys."

Stunned, the Birthday Gang clung to the cement wall, staring at the stranger. Felix shook his head and blinked a few times to make sure he wasn't seeing things.

"We're listening," he rasped in as tough a voice as he could muster.

The stranger straightened the cuffs of his jacket. He was a snappy dresser, to say the least. His silver suit jacket was worn over an expensive, black dress shirt whose sleeves ended in gold cuff links, and he wore a purple necktie.

"I hear you and your boys have been having walrus problems."

Felix felt a dozen eyes lock onto him. The gang was looking to him for leadership. "Yes," Felix said, inching closer. "I've roughed up plenty of folks in my time, but I've never seen anyone like the Black Walrus. He took us out like we were roaches in a bug spray factory."

"You just need the right leader." The strange intruder sat on the edge of the card table and crossed one of his legs over the opposite knee. "Somebody with spunk and moxie. Somebody like the Walrus ... somebody cut from the same cloth." The newcomer straightened his tie.

"And that's you, I suppose?" Felix asked.

The stranger blew a smoke ring and nodded. "In exchange for your help, I'll take care of your walrus problem and let you have your way with this burg. Be my right-hand man." The smoke ring drifted down from the table and onto the floor, where it broke.

"Our help doing what? What do you want?"

Chuckling, the stranger opened his arms. "I want the whole enchilada. Don't get me wrong, Cumpleaños, your little operation is cute, but once the Black Walrus is gone, I'm gonna run this town. Turn Cremini City into the center of a new criminal empire. Interested?"

Felix glanced around the inside of the cell. "I don't see that we have much of a choice." The stranger grinned, put down the keys, picked up his laser tommy gun, and blasted off the cell's lock. The door creaked open.

As Felix stepped out of the cell to shake the stranger's small hand, he stumbled over the garbage bag. The bag moaned.

"Just a guest," the would-be crime boss said, raising his eyebrow ridges in response to Felix's surprise. "Excuse me for a moment."

He hopped off the table and untied the top of the bag. Inside was a man wearing a singed lab coat full of burn holes, his face bruised and his eyes covered by broken goggles. As his new leader dragged the man out of the bag, Felix saw that the captive's hair was frazzled and singed, as well.

The tiny stranger held the smoldering meat stick between his paw toes and blew a mouthful of smoke into his captive's face, his tail wagging.

"Say hello to the future of Cremini City, Dr. Thorium."

"Please ...," the battered scientist coughed, "I'm sorry, Floofles ... I ...."

"I always hated that name!" The tough-talking Chihuahua grabbed his tommy gun and walked on his hind legs toward the doorway.

"Well, what should we call you?" Felix asked as he and the Birthday Gang followed the Chihuahua out.

The Chihuahua turned his head and smirked. "Lil' Poochy has a nice ring to it."

Chapter 16

Leaning back in her sticky leather chair and plopping her bare feet on the desk, Stevia Brinkles put her hands behind her head and relaxed. The overhead fan filled the whole place with the smell of pickle brine.

The desk in front of her was coated in brine stains and covered in a dozen empty pickle jars and one full one. There was an unsolved puzzle cube and a pile of pencils, which she'd organized into different shapes and patterns a dozen times.

The same old whup-whup-whup of the fan reminded Stevia of how much today had been like yesterday. And the day before that. And the day before that.

There just wasn't much to do as head of the zoo's Pinniped Department. After that incident with the hyperactive manatee and the turkey baster and the yoga pants, folks in Cremini City didn't want much to do with blubbery sea mammals.

Stevia yawned as she stretched her legs. Just as her eyes started to droop, she heard a knock at the door.

"Come in," she stammered, lowering her feet to the floor and brushing drops of brine off her "Pickles Rock! 1989 World Tour" tee shirt.

A brown-haired boy with thick glasses stepped into the office. "Afternoon, Ms. Brinkles," he said, crinkling his nose. "My name is Alex Portobello. I hate to interrupt your … uh … busy schedule, but I have a … business proposition for you."

Folding her hands, Stevia sat up straight. "Business proposition? You tryin' to sell me more stuffed giraffes? I already have, like, twenty-seven stuffed giraffes. I hate 'em!" She banged her fist on the desk, scattering the pencils.

"No, madam. Something much more benign." The young man slid the backpack off his shoulders and sat in a chair across from Stevia, putting one elbow and his forearm on the desk.

"I'd like after-hours access to the walrus enclosure. The 'behind the scenes' part of the walrus enclosure, if you know what I mean."

Stevia drew a pickle from the full jar and stroked her chin with it, thinking. "Seems pretty fishy to me. What would a youngster like you want with them walruses?"

"It's the space I'm interested in, Ms. Brinkles: it's inconspicuous, centrally-located, and spacious. The blubbery company is simply a bonus."

Stevia held the fat, dill pickle between her thumb and forefinger and stuck it between her teeth. There was something familiar about this boy. "You're that kid that messed with the sloths a couple years ago, aren't you?"

Alex scooted back in his chair and pushed his glasses up on his nose. "I, um … don't know what you're talking about. I didn't even know this zoo had sloths."

Squinting, Stevia leaned forward. "It is you, you ornery dill snapper! I can't believe they let you back into the zoo. And I'll bet you're up to something nasty like rubbin' Bengay on the penguins."

Alex frowned. "Ms. Brinkles, please. If you'll just let me explain—"

"Nothing doing, pal. There's no way I'm letting anybody just waltz into the walrus enclosure, least of all you with your weird ideas."

"But, Ms. Brinkles—"

"No buts." Stevia yanked the pickle out of her mouth and slammed it back into the open jar, "Now get out of my office before I call the—"

"You haven't even heard my offer yet." Alex hefted his backpack onto Stevia's desk, sending a few empty pickle jars clinking onto the floor. "I wouldn't ask for access to the walrus habitat without offering some sort of compensation."

Running her finger around the lip of the pickle jar, Stevia raised an eyebrow. "Compensation?"

The boy's gaze softened, and he smiled once again. "Yes, compensation. I've got something that's sure to pique your interest."

Stevia leaned back again and gripped the armrests of her chair. "All right, I'm listening."

"Did you know that, with the right technology and know-how, you can find some of the most interesting online forums?" Alex asked, unzipping his backpack.

"I hope you won't think less of me for this, but while exploring the Public Television forums last night, I came across the most interesting series of posts from a user called Picklelover17."

The zookeeper froze. Her face turned hot, and she felt sweat building on her forehead. "A certain series of posts about the latest episode of *The Painting of Joys with Bill Russ*," Alex continued.

Stevia's heartbeat quickened. "Bill Russ ...," she whispered, thinking of the afro-sporting, bearded TV painter.

"You're a fan, aren't you?" Alex said.

Stevia sighed. "The way he paints those happy little bushes ... it just makes me melt like butter. Bill Russ is the fire that ignites my womanly heart."

Alex smirked. "I thought as much."

Reaching into his backpack, Alex produced a curious-looking disc, which he slipped into Stevia's quivering hands. She could hardly believe her eyes: a mint-condition copy of *Bill Russ: A Life Well-Painted*!

"Where did you get this?! I've been scouring every convention and music festival for this disc for years. What do you want for it? I can give you, like, fifteen stuffed giraffes. I hate those things!"

Alex shouldered his backpack and stood. "Access to the walrus exhibit at my leisure will be plenty, Ms. Brinkles. A pleasure doing business with you."

"Yeah, yeah," Stevia mumbled, gently stroking the side of the disc and tossing a giant ring of keys at the boy. "Just lock up when you're done."

Chapter 17

Felix Cumpleaños and the Birthday Gang
arrived at the agreed-upon address, a small,
standalone, light gray office building. A sign
hung above the door that used to say "Thorium
Laboratories," but someone had plastered a giant
X over it. A wave of cool, smoky air hit Felix as
he and the Gang stepped into their new leader's
hideout.

There was a small sitting room just inside the
front door and a large room beyond it that
looked like, at one point, it could've been a
laboratory or something. Around the doorway
was a thick, metal frame and huge hinges that
could've supported a steel door.

Felix noticed a few pipes jutting from the
walls of the smaller room and large electrical
outlets like something you'd plug a stove or

fridge into. Maybe this room used to be a kitchen.

It had dark red walls which, about halfway down, were coated in mahogany paneling and a series of tiled, diamond-shaped pieces of yellow glass. When he looked closely, Felix saw burn marks through the glass, as if the entire facility had been badly damaged and then rebuilt in a hurry.

Spotless, dark green carpet covered the floor. Two couches with green upholstery lined the small room. Dim, moody lighting illuminated the place.

On one side of the room stood a jukebox, which softly played smooth, relaxing jazz and swing tunes from the '20s and '30s.

Felix took a seat on the couch, which squeaked. The couch looked old, a style that wasn't manufactured anymore, but the leather was clearly new. Gary and Piñata Pete sat next to him while the rest of the gang stood around, looking at their feet and taking in the sights and smells of the strange building.

"Well, don't just sit there like a bunch of saps," said a squeaky voice from inside the larger part of the facility. "Step into my office."

Felix stood and walked through a cloud of smoke and into the large main room. He tried to hide his shock. The room reminded him of nightclubs he'd only seen in magazines. Magazines from about a hundred years ago.

The walls and floor were the same as the sitting room. In one corner near the door leading to the smaller room sat a set of chairs similar to the couch in the entryway.

A pool table, complete with sixteen balls and long, wooden cues, stood near one of the walls. Along the other wall was a jet-black counter, complete with bar stools and with a huge shelf behind it.

A golden chandelier with dozens of lights and crystals hung from the ceiling. A huge rug with a complex, colorful pattern lay in the middle of the room. Felix and the gang strode across the rug and approached the desk against the far wall.

He and his goons sat in the series of office chairs in front of the desk. The desk was made of mahogany like the wall panels. The front, which faced Felix, was covered in intricate carvings, but Felix was sure the other side contained all kinds of drawers and compartments.

A rectangle of green felt covered the desk-top to keep it safe from damage, and an army of golden fountain pens stood in a crystal holder, ready for use.

Lil' Poochy sat behind the desk in a wooden chair with red upholstery more than seven times as big as he was. He sat on a pile of six pillows, which allowed him to see over the desk. His lower limbs, the ones he walked upright on like human legs, were stretched out atop the desk. In one of his upper paws, he held a fresh, smoldering cigar.

"Welcome to my humble abode, boys," said Lil' Poochy, blowing smoke out his tiny nostrils. "Glad you decided to accept my offer to help you deal with the Black Walrus."

"Don't mention it," Felix said. He waved his hand in front of his face to get rid of some of the smoke. "Nice place."

"You like it? It's just a temporary headquarters, somewhere to hang my hat until I start running this burg. You boys want some cigars?"

"We're good, thanks," Felix stated. "You know those things'll kill you, right?"

Lil' Poochy chuckled. "These are my own, special recipe. No tobacco. Just dried bacon and ham shavings."

Felix wasn't sure if it was nerves or the fact that he was talking to a Chihuahua in a suit and tie, but something about Lil' Poochy made him uneasy. He wanted to keep this visit as short as possible. "How did you afford this place?" he said, trying to change the subject.

The stylish Chihuahua snickered. "Let's just say it's amazing how much cabbage you can make selling a few high-tech inventions and a bunch of experimental research on the black market. Now, let's get down to business."

Lil' Poochy extinguished his smoking meat stick in a golden ashtray and stood on all fours, resting his front paws on the desk.

He leaned forward. "I ain't had human-level intelligence for long—I didn't have the best ... processing skills when I was just a plain, old Chihuahua—but I've had my smarts long enough to have the Walrus figured. He's playing hero."

"Playing?" Felix inquired.

"Think about it, compadre. Who'd be crazy enough to strap on a spandex jumpsuit and try to be a real-life costumed hero? We're not dealing with some rogue cop or public servant.

"The Walrus is just a weirdo who's read one too many comic books to keep one foot in reality, and he cares too much about 'innocent civilians' to know what's good for him."

Lil' Poochy lowered his teeny, fuzzy head and chortled. "All we have to do is introduce him to some real-world consequences. Right now, he's patrolling the streets because that's helping the city with its crime problem.

"If he has to choose between parading around in colorful underwear and keeping people safe, it'll shatter his confidence. And that's—" Lil' Poochy raised one of his front paws and drew in two toes, forming a pistol shape and making a firing motion "—when we rub him out."

Felix squinted his eyes and shook his head. "I still don't follow."

"You will. You and the boys just have to trust me. For now, we have some work to do."

The canine mob boss pushed himself away from the desk and stood on the chair. Reaching down, he pulled one of the desk drawers open. He grabbed a rolled-up sheet of paper in his teeth, which he set on top of the desk. With one, swift motion of his front paws, he unfurled the paper.

It was a map of Cremini City and the surrounding area. Lil' Poochy pointed to a road just outside the city. "At around one o'clock tomorrow afternoon, an armored military truck will be passing through Cremini City on this road. We just have to intercept the truck and make off with its cargo."

Felix pulled back. "You want us to rob a military vehicle? Why?"

"I just told you: to beat the Black Walrus, we need to demoralize him. Show him that when he hits us, we'll hit back twice as hard." Lil' Poochy raised one of his eyebrow ridges. "And to hit back, we're gonna need some serious firepower."

Felix swallowed. "Isn't going after a military transport a little dangerous, even for us?"

The devious pup threw his head back and barked a high-pitched, piercing laugh. "You ain't small-time hoodlums no more, Felix. You're running with Lil' Poochy now. And Lil' Poochy don't go after anything but the big scores."

Chapter 18

A tiny bell rang as Alex entered McPorkburger. The familiar smell of lard-soaked beef greeted him as he made his way across the tile floor. The chattering of the crowd echoed off the small building's walls. He almost plugged his ears.

About fifty conversations were going on at once. It was around 2 p.m., long after the lunch rush, but Alex had never seen McPorkburger so packed.

"Over here, Alex."

Tracy stood and waved from a booth. As Alex weaved in and out of the crowd and pushed his way past a few particularly large individuals, he thought about the deodorant he'd put on that morning.

Maybe, he thought, instead of trying to smell good, as his mom suggested, he should do his best to smell utterly repulsive. It'd take care of the problem of crowds and at the same time repulse the forces of crime. Maybe there was a way to squeeze the stink juice out of a skunk like toothpaste from a tube ....

"Alex, come on. The meeting's about to start."

Snapped back to reality, Alex slid into the booth next to Tracy and Brian. Leslie and Joe sat across from them.

"Hello, Brian," Alex said, "How's that toe jam mustard sitting?"

"Not well," Brian answered, grasping his stomach.

Alex hadn't ordered food, but he guessed the pile of burgers, fries, popplers, fried pork sandwiches, and fish bricks on buns in the middle of the table would be more than enough for all of them.

The smell of fried ... everything ... was intense. Alex hadn't seen such a scrumptious bounty since the giant pudding and herring feast he'd prepared last Thanksgiving.

With a thump, Brian hefted a giant black notebook with a huge stack of loose paper jammed inside it onto the table, scattering a few fries. Brian rose and stood on the booth seat. He stuck two fingers in his mouth and whistled, bringing the chattering around him to a halt.

"Welcome, everybody," Brian said, spreading his arms wide. "Welcome to the first meeting of the Black Walrus Fan Club."

A shiver worked its way up Alex's spine. At first, he thought he'd attend the meeting just to do some reconnaissance and measure his reputation with the public. But after hearing Brian say it, it finally hit him: he had a fan club!

The crowd roared with clapping and cheers of "The Black Walrus rocks!" and "I want the Black Walrus to kiss my schnauzer!"

After the applause died down, Brian opened the notebook and pulled a sheet of paper from the pocket inside the front cover. Alex caught a glimpse of a few of the pages inside.

They showed a rough sketch of his crime-fighting uniform based on the description that the lady he'd saved two weeks ago had given the police. Surprisingly accurate, Alex thought, although the sketched figure was quite a bit more muscular than he was, and its face didn't have the smoothness of one who regularly treated his skin with a mixture of paprika and Tibetan panda mucus.

Brian continued. "First order of business: I feel strongly that the Black Walrus needs a theme song. Something they can play on the news broadcasts when they talk about his exploits. Any ideas?"

A woman near the deep fryer raised her grease-stained hand. "It should be a rock song. Like a classic rock song."

"No, R&B," shouted someone else near the trash cans.

"I can get started on something," said a bearded man as he stood up from a stool near one of the counters.

Alex's jaw dropped, and the chewed-up pork sandwich inside almost fell out. That was M.C. Pooperdunk, the owner of the Groovy Pelican, Cremini City's hippest dance club. "I'm thinking sort of a classic rock/R&B/techno mix."

Alex straightened his back and swallowed, puffing out his chest a little. He knew heroes were supposed to be humble public servants, but he couldn't help it. M.C. Pooperdunk—*the* M.C. Pooperdunk—was writing his theme song!

"Excellent," Brian said. "On to the next order of business: the Black Walrus' secret identity."

Alex shifted and grimaced. He hadn't expected this to come up.

"I know we don't want to blow his cover," Brian continued, "but at the same time, we're all curious. So any theories we have don't leave this restaurant. Understood?"

The crowd nodded and mumbled in agreement.

Tracy spoke up. "The Black Walrus would have to be someone heroic, someone already trying to help people out. I'll bet he's a soldier or a fireman or something."

"I'm afraid you're wrong on that account, little lady," said a voice from the booth across from Tracy's.

Alex caught the smell of pickles. He turned to his left, and his jaw dropped again. There was the rounded, brine-speckled form of zookeeper Stevia Brinkles. She was the only one on her side of the booth. There was a pile of about forty cheeseburgers, all with their top buns removed, and a stack of picked-off pickle chips sat in front of her. She waved at Alex and smiled.

"The Black Walrus' fighting style isn't like anything you'd see in a police or military training program," she explained, "and he's too short to be a firefighter."

"Maybe a counselor or a therapist?" suggested a McPorkburger employee near the milkshake machine. "Someone who sees a lot of people who need to talk about their problems. Anyone who sees that many people in distress is bound to want to help out. Fight depression and anxiety on a grand scale."

Alex couldn't hide his confusion. Stevia placed a pickle chip on her tongue and chewed it slowly. She shook her head. "Not a bad guess, but no. No counselor would refer to himself as 'the Crispy Bacon of Vengeance' and disappear into the night after he fights evildoers. Someone like that would stick around and talk to the civilians he saved."

Drumming his fingers on the table, Alex cleared his throat. He studied Ms. Brinkles' face. The restaurant had grown quiet; even the sound of people munching their deep-fried shortening on a stick had died away.

"He seems like he'd be someone who was tired of his job," said a mustached man in a polo shirt. "Some pencil pusher bored with the daily grind and water cooler talk. And he'd have to be a homeowner. Realistically, you couldn't hide crime-fighting gadgets from roommates or even landlords."

Ms. Brinkles snickered as she lifted the top bun off another cheeseburger. She peeled two pickles off the meat patty and placed them in her pile.

"Not necessarily. You'd be surprised what you can hide in a closet or under a bed, even in a crowded apartment or a bedroom. Heck, a guy like the Black Walrus probably even knows how to install a secret compartment in his living space."

Alex made sure no one was looking and wiped the sweat from his forehead with a napkin. He started thinking of excuses to leave the fan club meeting, maybe something about how Brian's musk was overpowering him (he'd used that excuse to get out of gym class more than a few times.) But no. He had to stick around to see how this ended.

A muffled cough echoed off the restaurant walls. A lady in a Hawaiian shirt strode up to Ms. Brinkles' table and set her milkshake on the edge. "Stevia," she said, "if I didn't know any better, I'd think you knew who the Walrus really was."

"Oh, heck no," Stevia said, waving her hand at the woman as she wiped her lips. "I just like kicking around theories, that's all. When you're stuck placing orders for manatee food all day, you have a lot of time to think. That is, when you're not being distracted by the … abnormal noises that have been coming from the walrus enclosure for about a week and a half."

A knot formed in Alex's stomach.

"Well, you've given us a lot to think about," said Brian as he scratched his face. He clearly sensed the tension in the room. "Let's move on to the next item on the agenda: the cosplay contest!"

Alex wasn't sure how to feel about the series of homemade Black Walrus costumes; one of the fan club members had painted half a cantaloupe black, cut out eye holes, and plopped it on his head.

But it was getting hard to concentrate on the meeting itself. After hearing Ms. Brinkles' comments, Alex was in a daze. Once Brian declared the meeting over, Alex rose from his seat and marched toward the door, once again pushing his way through the crowd.

His excitement over having his own fan club had evaporated like grape juice out of a sunbathing macaque's navel. Getting permission before using the walrus enclosure had been the right thing to do, but it may have left him open to discovery.

He'd have to keep a close eye on Stevia Brinkles.

Chapter 19

Felix felt sweat building up beneath his coat and the band of his hat. He'd hoped the boulder would provide some shade for he and the gang, but it was the wrong time of day. The sun was hitting the side of the boulder they crowded behind. The huge rock only accentuated the sun's rays and was cooking Felix like an egg. His fedora and overcoat weren't exactly helping.

That morning, they'd hiked out of town and past the sign that said, "Just a few miles to Cremini City: Home of the World's Biggest Ball of Bellybutton Lint." They now stood behind a boulder on one side of one of the only roads leading into the city.

Felix looked around at the rest of the gang. Gary was panting while trying to keep his breathing as quiet as possible. He leaned forward and put his hands on his knees, clenching his eyes shut as drops of sweat wormed their way beneath the brim of his purple party hat and down his face, splatting on the dirt beneath him.

Lil' Poochy shot Gary an annoyed look and growled.

Felix had been around the talking Chihuahua for a few days now, so he figured the creature who commanded him should've seemed a little less strange. But Lil' Poochy kept surprising him.

He was agile and resilient. While the entire Birthday Gang had huffed and puffed on their hike to the outskirts of Cremini City, the tiny dog had trotted bouncingly at the head of the pack like he didn't have a care in the world.

The whole way, he'd carried a black suitcase in his teeth. He hadn't told Felix or any of the gang what was inside, and the suitcase now sat safely on the ground at the weird canine's feet.

As soon as they'd reached the rock outcropping, Lil' Poochy had pulled his tommy gun from its holster on his back and hadn't loosened his grip on it since. Felix followed the dog's gaze to the middle of the road where the sprinkle-covered, pink cupcake sat.

The gang had set up the cupcake and candle an hour or so ago and since then had been ready for their target to arrive.

A bead of sweat ran down Felix's back. Just as he was about to speak up about the heat, he heard an engine. A big engine.

He peeked around the side of the rock. Just as Lil' Poochy had predicted, an armored military vehicle was making its way toward the cupcake. It slowed to a stop as it approached the dangerous baked good.

Felix heard the back doors of the truck fly open and slam shut again as a Kevlar-clad platoon surrounded the cupcake and bent down to examine it. One of them, probably an explosives specialist, flipped a kit open and gingerly picked up the cupcake.

At a nod from Lil' Poochy, Felix reached into his coat and activated the ignition device.

A spark flew from the cupcake's candle-like fuse and began to sizzle. The soldier dropped the device, jumped back, and shouted for his squad to take cover. But before they could turn away, the cupcake exploded in a shower of fire and frosting.

Each member of the platoon flew through the air, then landed on the asphalt, skidding across the hard ground. The front of the truck got the worst of the blast, and a spider web crack spread across its windshield.

"Now's our chance, boys!" Lil' Poochy squeaked.

He hopped into action. With agility Felix never would have expected from a tiny canine, the Chihuahua hopped onto the truck's hood and pointed the business end of his laser tommy gun squarely at the driver.

Felix and the rest of the gang dashed out from behind the boulder and menaced the recovering soldiers with their weapons. The scattered squad stood and put their hands up.

"Afternoon, gentlemen," Lil' Poochy said to the driver, who was more flabbergasted than scared. "We've come to relieve you of your cargo. Now personally, I prefer to do things the easy and civilized way, but if you'd rather ...."

The Chihuahua pressed the barrel of his weapon against the windshield. The two men in the armored truck's cab glanced at each other and put their hands in the air. At Lil' Poochy's command, they stepped out of the truck and fell to their knees.

"Smart move, fellas," the snappily dressed canine sneered. "Felix, Pete, come with me to the back of the truck. The rest of you, tie these blockheads up and keep them covered. And make sure you swipe their radios and phones so they can't call for backup."

Felix wiped the sweat from beneath his fedora and holstered his confetti cannon as Lil' Poochy hopped down from the hood of the truck, stowed the tommy gun on his back, gripped the handle of the black suitcase in his teeth, and dropped to all fours, bouncing to the back of the armor-clad truck and wagging his tail.

Felix's throat had gone dry. He'd never dreamed he and the Birthday Gang would ever do anything like rob an armored truck, let alone a military vehicle. Lil' Poochy was either a criminal genius or a lunatic. Or worse, both.

One of the guards opened the truck's rear door and stepped back. Piñata Pete and Felix rounded the bumper and peered through the open doors.

Inside was an army-green, cylinder-shaped object with a pointed tip on one end and a jet booster on the other. A series of metal stands and a web of tie-down straps secured it to the truck floor. Felix dropped his jaw and took a step back.

"Is that a mini-missile?!"

"Observant as always, Felix my boy," Lil' Poochy said, popping open the black suitcase. He pulled out three glasses, a tiny bucket of ice, a pair of ice tongs, and a bottle of liquid with a label featuring two strips of bacon and Lil' Poochy's grinning face.

Felix blinked hard a few times just to convince himself he was really stealing a missile. "I ... I thought you were building a criminal empire. I thought we'd be knocking over banks and running protection rackets—standard stuff. What the frosting are we going to do with a missile?"

"Can't make an omelet without causing catastrophic property damage." Lil' Poochy handed Felix and Pete two full glasses and stored the empty bottle inside his suit jacket. "Now, I think we have time for a little celebration before we unload this keen piece of equipment. Once we get it back to the warehouse, the Black Walrus is as good as out of our fur."

Felix cleared his throat. He heard the ice in Pete's glass jingle as his friend's hand shook. "Look, Lil' Poochy, I appreciate your busting us out of the clink and everything. But I think that maybe ... launching a missile inside Cremini City ... it's a little much for common criminals like us, and—"

The dog shook his tiny head and chuckled. His pointed canine teeth were showing.

"Felix, Felix, Felix ... You still don't understand what's happening to your little city, do you? With cats like the Black Walrus patrolling the streets, you can't just menace store owners and snatch purses anymore. You have to think bigger. Much bigger."

The smile fell from Lil' Poochy's face, and he fixed his teeny, black eyes on Felix. "I'll be carrying on with my plan with or without your little gang, Felix. And when my scheme's complete, every lowlife in Cremini City will answer to me. So, whose side do you want to be on?"

Felix swallowed the lump in the back of his throat. "Yours," he croaked.

Lil' Poochy smiled again. "Good. Finish your drinks, and let's get this thing back to headquarters. We're burnin' daylight."

With one swig, Felix drained his glass. He winced. It was some kind of liquified, carbonated bacon.

Chapter 20

At 4:23 p.m. (precisely), Alex flung the back door open and skipped into the kitchen. He took a deep breath. He'd had time to stop by the zoo on his way home, and finishing up his latest project had put him in a good mood. Besides, he remembered, he had a fan club.

"Is that taco soup, Mom?" he asked, pointing to the bubbling pot on the stove, "It smells fantastic."

"Oh. Yes, it is. Thanks, Alex. You're in a good mood this afternoon."

"Well, why shouldn't I be? The sun is shining, Dad bought a new TV, I made a deal with that hobo who lives in the dumpster behind the electronics store and got some more components for my inventions, and last night, I perfected the super-prunes. I've never been so regular, Mom."

"That's great." Gwen Portobello smiled cautiously. It was the same look she'd given Alex when he duct-taped the Jenkins' cat to a jet-powered Segway and tried to break the land speed record.

She sniffed the air and crinkled her nose. "Alex, you smell like livestock."

Alex froze, rubbing his palms on his pants. "What do you mean?"

"You smell like you've been around wild animals." She walked over to Alex and grabbed his wrists. "And your hands are filthy! They're covered in ... oil or something ... Alex, what have you been up to?"

"Uh ... I was ... giving a goat an oil massage." He was running low on excuses.

Mom straightened her mouth and breathed out through her nose. She studied Alex up and down. "Giving a goat an oil massage. Is that why you're home thirty-six minutes late?"

"Of course ... I mean ... do you know how long it takes Farmer Jenkins' goat to relax? There was so much tension in her hamstrings, Mom."

Alex's mom lowered her head and looked directly into her son's eyes. She clutched Alex's wrists a little tighter.

"I'm getting worried about you, Alex. I've said it before: you need to learn to communicate. You spend so much time in your room or out of the house doing heaven knows what that your father and I barely see you.

"A lot of parts of the city aren't safe. Did you know the neighbors saw that Black Walrus guy fight some nut in the middle of the street? Our street! And because of your ... interests, I can't be sure whether or not that story about massaging a goat is true or if you're trying to hide something. And I don't know which would be worse."

Alex yanked his wrists out of his mom's hands. "All right. I wasn't massaging a goat. I was working on a project. I don't see what the big deal is, Mom. I know I don't have many friends, but I'm just trying to help people. Like that poor, stressed-out goat who really could use a massage or that kid in fourth grade who told me he wanted a third nostril."

Alex's mom sank into a chair by the table and pressed her fingers to her forehead. "We promised never to bring up that incident with little Timmy tri-nostrils again, remember? I just don't see why you can't—"

"My inventions have a ton of potential." Alex's face grew hot. "I know I don't always pay attention in school and that I ruined Christmas last year when I accidentally irradiated the ham and that I'm not exactly the kind of kid that you and Dad were when you were my age, but my creations could change the world. Why can't you just accept me for who I am?"

Mom's look softened, and she set her hands on her knees. "Alex, you know we'll always love you and accept you for exactly who you—"

"Is that why you're always threatening to ship me off to boarding school?"

Alex trudged into the living room and started up the stairs. "I'm going upstairs to take a shower. Since, apparently, my aroma offends. And then I'm going to my room to finish the interspecies communication device."

"The what?"

Alex sighed. "Never mind, Mom. You wouldn't understand. You never understand."

After a quick shower, Alex went straight to his room and shut the door. He tossed his backpack on the bed and knelt by his bedside.

Reaching beneath the bed and past the collection of hardened gum he'd shaped into different members of the Canadian parliament, he pulled out a cardboard box full of newspaper clippings and printouts of news websites.

As he scanned the papers, he was greeted by headlines that read "Black Walrus Rescues Woman from Infamous Birthday Gang," "The Black Walrus: Guardian of Cremini City," and "Black Walrus: Masked Hero or Subversive Spandex Marketing Campaign?" He closed his eyes and straightened his back.

His place was in skin-tight spandex defending the city and its inhabitants, not squabbling with Mom and Dad or Ms. Grunderson or other people who didn't even know how to properly operate a custard-powered crossbow.

Alex shoved the box back under his bed and glanced around his room. His accomplishments were all around him; the heroics of the Black Walrus had even made the smell from his failed cabbage solar panel experiment less noticeable.

Slinking to the closet, Alex shifted a piece of wood next to the sliding doors to reveal a rectangular, metal panel. Flipping the panel upward to access the new electronic keypad, he entered his code.

Like a pair of grocery store doors, the wooden closet doors slid to the side. Piles of wrinkled clothes had been jammed into the closet's corners to make room for the black cape, blue body suit, brown chest piece with white tusks, and gold gloves, boots, and belt, which adorned a steel mannequin in the middle of the closet, ready for action.

He'd made a few alterations to his crime-fighting armory since the incident with the Birthday Gang. A pair of tiny syringes now sat on the inside of the mask in two pockets just above the cheeks.

The syringes contained a minor paralysis toxin Alex had mixed up during English class. If anyone tried to remove his mask, they'd feel a prick and their arm would go numb.

He'd also added an extra layer of temperature-resistant material to the body suit and cape, which would allow him to function efficiently whether it was as hot as a sweat lodge full of fresh-from-the-oven pies or cold as a troop of shaved poodles on an ice-skating rink.

He'd attached a liquid cheese dispenser to the utility belt, constructed a communication signal jammer inside the tusks, and modified a walrus bobble head to dispense soothing, moisturizing lotion from its eye sockets. After all, you can't dispatch the forces of evil without baby-smooth skin.

And now it was time to add another weapon to his arsenal. Alex pulled a piece of folded notebook paper from his pocket and unfolded it. He grabbed the squishy, brown chest piece and flipped it over, revealing a motherboard covered in computer chips, ports, and wires.

Alex sat in his computer chair with the chest piece in his lap. The only sound he could hear was the soft splattering of rain on the glass of the closed window. Glancing from the notebook paper to the chest piece and back again, he used a tiny screwdriver to adjust the components ever so slightly.

At last, he unzipped the top portion of his backpack and produced the final component: a mystacial vibrissae (or "whisker") from a real walrus.

Carefully, like he was surgically removing the appendix of a rabid mole, he threaded the whisker in and out of the ports and clamps of the chest piece, screwing it in place. It was delicate work. By the time he finished, it was dark outside.

He put the cape and suit back on its mannequin stand in the closet and attached the upgraded chest piece to the front, standing back to admire his work. Another crime-fighting device complete. He entered the code on the keypad, and the closet doors slid shut.

* * *

"You ready to begin the broadcast, Boss?" Felix asked as he ran the microphone cord along a side wall to keep it out of the shot.

The fluorescent lights illuminated the office surprisingly well, and the acoustics of the empty warehouse room were fantastic.

Gary had finally finished setting up the camera. Dozens of wires snaked across the cement floor on the top level of the warehouse and into to a laptop. Cold night air seeped in from an open window on the other side of the room, and Felix and Pete stood on either side of a desk, holding their streamer cannons aloft like a couple of Buckingham Palace guards.

"Yes," said a high-pitched voice. "The seven-o-clock news broadcast is about half over now. It's time to teach Cremini City how to sit and stay before its new master."

Chapter 21

"Alex, come quick!"

Mom sounded scared. Scrambling, Alex leapt from his chair, tossed open the door to his room, and dashed to the stair railing. He half-expected to see a group of vengeful hamster arsonists setting fire to the carpet, but his parents were just sitting on the couch staring at the new TV in silence.

Alex took a breath and rushed down the stairs as he listened to the TV.

"This is Max Blatherson with breaking news. Just a few minutes ago, our broadcast was pirated, and we viewed some troubling amateur footage, which included a message intended for the mysterious Black Walrus.

"For those who missed it, we'll be airing the footage again, but we caution that those of you disturbed by party favors or talking animals may want to turn off your television sets."

There was a burst of static followed by footage of two men standing in what looked like an abandoned warehouse holding streamer cannons and standing on either side of a red leather swivel chair, which faced away from the camera. The Birthday Gang!

Florescent lighting illuminated the room, but the camera was angled so that it didn't reveal too much of the warehouse interior.

"Hey there, Black Walrus," said a squeaky voice from the other side of the chair, "I've been speaking to my good friends in the Birthday Gang, and they told me you gave them quite a walloping a week or so ago. Well, I'm somebody who knows his onions, and I think I can help you and these boys resolve your differences."

The chair spun around, revealing a Chihuahua in a silver suit jacket, a black dress shirt, and a purple tie. The same Chihuahua that had scared Mrs. Crumpleston when Alex had fought the scientist in the middle of the street. It sat upright with a smirk on its face, holding a red-brown cigar in one paw.

"I had the chair brought in for dramatic effect. Thought you'd appreciate that."

The Chihuahua crossed his lower legs and leaned back in the chair.

"The name's Lil' Poochy, former flea breeding ground and current criminal mastermind. You see, my blubbery friend, you can't just hit the criminal element like you did and not expect them to hit back twice as hard. You've sent these boys a clear message: either the Birthday Gang goes or you do."

Cold sweat formed on Alex's cheeks.

The weird canine hopped down from the chair and strolled to his right. The camera followed Lil' Poochy and revealed a mini-missile the size of an obese wiener dog.

Alex's stomach dropped. The rocket was mounted on a ramp and pointed out the warehouse window.

"There's no point in trying to locate us, Walrus; we're in the warehouse district, and you'd have to search through dozens of huge facilities to find us. It'd be like trying to find one piece of dry kibble in a sea of wet. I'm a reasonable canine, so I'm gonna give you a choice: either tell all of Cremini City who you really are and stop your little war on crime ...."

The camera panned backward and angled downward so it showed the screen of a nearby laptop. On the laptop's screen was an apartment-looking building. The building had a billboard-like sign near the roof that featured the cartoon heads of an old woman, a young boy, and a cartoon cat. Each of them had a sad face and huge, cute eyes.

"... or I'll fire this missile straight into the Cremini City Home for Widows, Orphans, and Crippled Kitties!"

Alex grimaced and stepped back. He stumbled against the stairs but kept his eyes glued to the television.

"My merry partygoers are welding the Home's doors and windows shut as we speak, so there's no way those sweet old ladies and parentless little urchins can get out. And if any cops show up, I launch the missile early."

Lil' Poochy snapped the toes on his front left paw. Felix Cumpleaños handed him an ashtray, and the talking Chihuahua extinguished his cigar. "You have two hours, Black Walrus. Choose wisely."

The video feed cut out, and Alex was left staring at Max Blatherson. He couldn't focus on whatever the newscaster was saying. He glanced at Mom, who'd scooted closer to Dad on the couch. She was blinking a lot and looked anxious.

"It's awful, Walt," she said. "What's happening to this city? It was bad enough when we just had to avoid certain parts of town, but then all the kids started idolizing a vigilante and now lives are in danger. How's it going to affect Alex? He already spends so much time away from home."

Walter Portobello cocked his head toward the stairs. "Alex, come here, please."

Staring at his shoes, Alex stepped into the living room and joined his parents on the couch. The air wheezed out of the cushion under his weight.

"Son, you know that this Black Walrus stuff isn't a game, right?"

"What do you mean, Dad?"

"Well, I know a lot of kids your age look up to this Walrus character, but his antics have put the city in real danger. Keeping secrets from the whole city ... taking the law into his own hands

... I know he's fighting criminals and trying to do good, but he's treating our city like a playground.

"And now his actions have threatened real people. There are—" Dad choked and cleared his throat. "There are a lot of people who could die tonight."

Alex's stomach felt like it was full of icy slugs. He kept looking at his feet. "Uh ... yeah, Dad. Yeah, I know what the Walrus does is dangerous."

Alex's mom sighed. "Well, I hope so. I worry about who you're looking up to."

Alex's skin turned dry and sticky. "I'm ... I'm going to go out on the porch for a while. Get some fresh air."

Trudging out the front door, Alex shut it behind him and began pacing on the porch. The smell of wet, after-the-rain asphalt filled his nostrils as the splapp-splapp-splapp of his sneakers against the concrete echoed in the quiet night. From inside, he could still hear his parents talking:

"He seems pretty bothered by this, Walt. I think Alex really does look up to that vigilante."

"Well, we've done our best to raise a good kid. That's really all we can do, isn't it?"

Alex clenched his eyes shut and massaged his forehead. He felt as torn as a couch covered in barbecue sauce sitting in the middle of a pride of lions.

"Is this my fault?" he mumbled to himself, putting his finger to his chin. "No, it can't be. The Birthday Gang was around long before I slapped on the spandex."

He paced faster. "And I don't even know how that Chihuahua from a few days ago turned into that Lil' Poochy thing. I didn't create it. At least ... I don't think I did ... unless the Birthday Gang really did turn to him because of the Black Walrus ... I mean, I guess if I'd helped Mrs. Crumpleston and captured the Chihuahua, this never would have happened."

Alex quit his pacing, leaned with his back against the door, and slid down until he plopped onto the cold concrete.

"I never wanted to hurt anyone. I just wanted to use my inventions. I just wanted to help people and have some fun while doing it ... I ...."

He took off his glasses and sank his head into his hands.

The groovy sounds of Johnny Meatball and the Porkettes shattered the silence: Alex's ringtone. He wiped his nose on his sleeve and took his phone out of his pocket.

The call came from an unknown number, and the caller ID picture showed a painting of an arctic landscape hanging in someone's living room. The painting didn't look professional, but it was still pretty good.

"Hello?" Alex answered, his voice cracking.

"Hey, Portobello," said a familiar voice. Alex could almost smell the pickles over the phone. "I take it you saw that video on the news?"

"Ms. Brinkles? How did you get my phone number?"

"Basic online database research." Alex heard a wet crunch. "You just gotta know where to look. I have the president of Japan's number, too. Guy really has a thing for Kosher dills. Anyway, what's your plan?"

Alex raised an eyebrow. "What do you mean, 'plan?' I don't know what you're—"

"You think I'm stupid or something? You come into my section of the zoo talking about wanting to use the walrus enclosure for something right after a walrus-themed hero hits the streets, and you don't expect me to connect the dots?"

Alex's heart skipped a little at the word "hero."

"So, what's your plan?"

"What plan?"

"Your plan to deal with that smart-mouthed dog. You've got to do something. That Poochy guy kind of reminds me of a stuffed giraffe. And you know how I feel about those little buggers."

Alex sniffed. He hung his head and let out a long sigh. "I ... I was thinking of just going to the news station and telling them who I am. There's no sense putting peoples' lives in danger."

"You can't do that! You think Lil' Poochy or the Birthday Gang wouldn't be threatening people if you'd sat your delicate little hiney on the ottoman and done nothing? They'd be terrorizing this city unchecked."

Alex ran his fingers over his scalp and felt the roots of his hair. "But I think I may have made a mistake. Trying to play hero and everything."

"Yeah, *playing* hero would've been a mistake. You're not pláying." Alex heard the slosh of brine and another juicy crunch. "Besides, heroes are allowed to make mistakes. And heroes are allowed to ask for help."

Perking his head up, Alex looked at the city skyline. He thought about all the Cremini-ites huddled around their TVs, paralyzed by the villainous Chihuahua's threat.

He thought about Tracy and Brian and all his other classmates who looked up to the Black Walrus. He thought about the panic at the Home for Widows, Orphans, and Crippled Kitties and all the malnourished, weak-kneed cats staggering around on their little crutches.

He clenched his fist and stood up.

"You're right. I can't let this stand." Alex's voice grew deeper, and he cleared his throat. "I am the oversized globule of peanut butter that sticks to the roof of the Mouth of Villainy. Lil' Poochy can't pry me free so easily.

"Ms. Brinkles, I need to get to the walrus enclosure. I don't have the equipment at my house to properly analyze the video footage or locate that furry scoundrel."

"All right! What's your address? I'll stop by and pick you up."

Alex glanced at his phone. Lil' Poochy had given him two hours to turn himself in. He'd spent five minutes moping on the porch, so he set a timer for one hour and fifty-five minutes. "There's no time. I'll meet you there."

"But how are you going to get to the zoo?"

Alex pushed his glasses higher onto his nose as a smile spread across his jaw. "I am the one-size-too-small briefs that squeeze the buttocks of evil. I have my ways."

Chapter 22

Alex flung open the front door and raced up the stairs toward his bedroom.

"Are you okay, son?" Dad asked.

"Never better, Dad," Alex replied, turning his head and looking back down the stairs to the living room couch. "I feel more refreshed than a gnome dipped in Listerine."

"Oh. That's ... nice." Dad furrowed his eyebrows and straightened his mouth, but he went back to watching the news.

Alex shut the door to his room and entered the code to open the closet. The doors slid back, revealing the suit and cape illuminated by a single ray of light. Slipping off his clothes, Alex zipped on the body suit, pulled on the shiny, yellow boots, stretched the golden gloves over his hands, and clipped his utility belt around his waist.

Using the new clamp feature on his right glove, he attached his phone to his wrist like a watch so he wouldn't need to keep reaching into his pocket to check the time. He fastened the plastic walrus muzzle onto his chest, attaching either side of the cape to the back of the chest piece to hold it in place.

Sliding the window open, he slipped the mask of the cowl over his eyes. The rain-drenched street below was quiet; the normal hustle and bustle of Cremini City was gone, and Alex didn't even hear the regular police sirens.

The city was scared.

Spotting the front yard tree out of the corner of his eye, Alex took a deep breath, placed his foot on the windowsill, and bounded outside.

Landing on a stout branch with his left foot, Alex launched himself toward the sidewalk and rolled as he hit the ground, transferring his momentum into a somersault. He rolled across the sidewalk and smacked against the door of his dad's car. His arm stung and he left a dent, but he hadn't caught his parents' attention.

Alex crawled to the front of the car and scanned the length of the block. For a moment, he thought, *I could jimmy open the car door, hot-*

wire the car, and drive it to the zoo. But he slapped the idea out of his head like a vengeful nun with a whacking ruler. The Black Walrus was no car thief.

He checked his phone. One hour and fifty-one minutes left. There had to be another way to get downtown in time.

Alex heard something coughing and hacking like a yak choking on a hairy pot roast. Mr. and Mrs. Crumpleston hobbled out of their house, staggering down the stairs of their front porch and toward their station wagon. Their joints popped and creaked more than the wooden floors at the annual Indoor Rhinoceros Riders Convention.

Of course! It was Tuesday night, and for the Crumplestons, that meant bingo night at the rec center.

Still crouched, the Black Walrus skittered across the street, careful to keep as much of his body as possible hidden under the black cape. He gripped the rear bumper of the Crumplestons' mustard-mixed-with-potting-soil yellow car whose entire frame was blotched with rust stains. Even on the outside, the car smelled like menthol rub and bunion ointment.

Bunion ointment of justice, Alex thought.

Gripping the rear bumper, he hoisted himself up and placed the bottoms of his feet against the bumper. He was perched like a gargoyle. Scarcely had he positioned himself than he felt a shaking and heard the car start up with a rickety "click-click-click-BLAM!"

They were off.

As usual, the Crumplestons shot out of the driveway and, pedal to the metal, flew down the road with the speed of an oiled-up cheetah wearing a jetpack. Over the rush of the wind, Alex heard Mr. Crumpleston's shouts of "Tell me I can't drive, will they?! Why, I'm as spry as I ever was! I'm not losing my memory or my grip on reality! Ain't that right, President Lincoln?"

Like a rock climber clutching a wall of stone, Alex inched to his right and peeked out from behind the rear of the car so he could see where they were going. The cowl's lenses protected the Black Walrus' eyes from the wind, just as he'd designed them to. He squinted as he tried to focus on the street signs zipping by.

The car began to pick up more and more speed. It was difficult, but he could see for a few miles down the road. He tried not to think about the asphalt speeding by underneath him, just waiting to tear his skin off should he slip and touch the ground.

Soon, the houses disappeared and gave way to a stream of streetlights. They were on the highway now, and the exit for the zoo was coming up.

Still gripping the bumper with his left hand, Alex drew one of the grapple guns from his belt. The car shielded the grappling pistol from the wind, but Alex still struggled to hold it straight.

He took a deep breath. He had to get the angle just right, or before he even got to try his hand at saving the day, he'd end up a boy-flavored, hairy pile of tapioca-consistency goop on the highway.

The exit sign flashed into view. He took the shot.

The grappling hook and cable whizzed through the air, hit its mark, and wrapped around the exit sign. Alex let go of the car's bumper and twisted his body around, whipping out from behind the car.

The grappling cable retracted and yanked him across the highway like he was a fishing lure and the exit sign was a fisherman with the reflexes of a ninja lemur.

The rush of wind from the other cars whizzing by almost blew him off course, and he nearly ran face-first into a semi-truck, but before he could say "I regret eating those salsa-and cheese-covered jelly doughnuts for lunch," Alex landed feet-first on the other side of the road.

He retracted the grapple gun's cable and slipped the device back in his belt. The zoo entrance was just across the parking lot.

He glanced at his wrist. One hour and twenty-six minutes left. He'd have to run.

He already felt like a tiny vacuum had sucked the air from his lungs, but there was no time for bellyaching. Alex took off. The empty zoo parking lot seemed to stretch on forever, and as he dashed through the zoo, Alex got a few confused looks from the kangaroo rats. At last, panting, he reached the walrus enclosure.

Ms. Brinkles was waiting for him and leaning against the bars with a pickle clenched in each fist.

* * *

"'Bout time you showed up," Stevia said, popping one of the pickles into her mouth. The cool pickle entrails oozed down her throat. "I was startin' to think you were actually scared of that Chihuahua."

"Fear is but a sunflower seed in the sea of hamsters that is my courage," the Black Walrus wheezed.

"Glad to hear it." Stevia plunged her hand into her back pocket and produced a set of keys. "Mosey your hamster ocean this way, and we'll go underneath the walrus exhibit."

"No need. I was thinking we'd take the express route."

Alex turned the "Atlantic Walruses" sign around, and a tiny section of the tallest rock face inside the enclosure fell away. A red laser beam shot from the opening. The spandex-clad lad stepped in front of the beam and let it scan his eye.

Stevia jumped as the concrete beneath them began to grind and shift, sinking in sections until it formed a cement stairway that led deep underground beneath the walrus enclosure.

Bowing a little, the Black Walrus held out his hand like a gentleman. Stevia took it, and he led her down the stone stairs. As they made their way down the narrow passageway, it grew darker and darker.

Stevia was used to all kinds of fish smells, but this hallway was particularly humid and stuffy, and the smell of half-eaten fish was strong even by her standards.

She put the other pickle in her mouth and sucked on it a little. The only sound was a series of familiar bellows echoing through the cavernous hallway.

The humidity abated a little as they reached the end of the passage. Alex flipped a switch and illuminated the dome-shaped, stadium-sized room at the end of the hallway.

The cave beneath the walrus enclosure had been expanded and now spread for hundreds of feet in every direction. Stevia guessed the cavern covered the underground of the whole city zoo. Sheets of cold rock formed what looked like a giant, multi-leveled series of stone patios.

On each level were all kinds of mechanical wonders: shelves and tables and racks holding ray guns, harpoon cannons, grappling hooks the size of watermelons, and nuclear-powered cotton candy makers.

Huge, silver canisters with tentacle-like wires sticking out of every side sat against one wall. There were pools of water of different sizes throughout the cavern, and in the center, she saw a long, black, steel table with a glowing top and a detailed map of Cremini City sprawled across it.

The stone ceiling stood several stories above them, and each wall had a computer monitor the size of a narwhal embedded in it. Every screen held the blueprint for a revolutionary new invention: a turbo-charged Zamboni or walrus-shaped mini submarine or some other fantastic machine.

The biggest monitor of all sat toward the middle of the room near the black table and had a keyboard in front of it that had more buttons and switches on it than Stevia's weird, smelly uncle had collectible troll figurines.

And there were walruses. The place was crawling with the blubbery sea mammals, at least ten times more than Stevia had ever seen at the zoo. They seemed completely at home with the adjustments to the cave, diving in and out of the pools, bellowing to each other, and sleeping in clumps.

Their smooth, fatty bodies flopped and slid around the technological wonders with ease. One relaxed in front of the computer, while another pressed a button on the wall with its flipper. A fish slid out of a secret compartment, and the walrus sucked it into its mouth.

The pickle dropped from Stevia's mouth with a plop. Alex smiled and gestured to the cavern. "Welcome to the Walrus Cave, Ms. Brinkles."

Chapter 23

Jogging across the rocky floor, the Black Walrus made his way to the middle of the cave and hopped onto the walrus lying in front of the computer. The walrus poked its head up and snuffled but didn't seem to mind being used as a chair.

"How'd you afford all this stuff?" Stevia asked, her mouth agape as she gazed around the cave.

"Online auctions," Alex answered. "You'd be surprised how much people are willing to pay for the world's first grape soda-powered jet ski."

"Aren't you cold?" Stevia massaged her upper arms.

"Not really. Thermal insulation was one of the first features I installed in the Black Walrus suit once I knew I'd be working down here. After all, I want my friends to be comfortable. Isn't that right, Jorge?" Alex rubbed the head of the walrus he was using as a seat.

His fingers flew across the keyboard as a series of program windows flashed on the screen. "Lil' Poochy may have thought himself clever by keeping his ultimatum short and revealing little of his location. But there's one facet of my crime-fighting arsenal he's underestimated: my memory. The two of us have met before."

Faster than Stevia's eyes could follow, Alex clicked through a series of windows featuring columns of numbers straight out of *The Matrix*, a three-dimensional map with a bunch of blue cubes, and a chicken in a tutu dancing like its life depended on it.

At last, Alex's fingers slowed, then stopped. A window that showed footage from a security camera appeared on the screen. It featured the outside of a suburban household. There was a black van in front of the house, and a Chihuahua and a man in a long lab coat hopped out of the vehicle. The man snatched a TV sitting on the curb.

The Black Walrus paused the video. "I may not know where that furry little devil is hiding, but I know someone who might. And I know how to find him.

"Last year, I designed a guidance program for my Swedish meatball delivery cannon. It used facial recognition to find someone's contact information: phone number, email address, et cetera. I intended to use it in conjunction with a lock-on system and high-powered cannon to guide meatballs like smart bombs and deliver them to whoever I desired.

"Unfortunately, the guidance program didn't work correctly. There was an unfortunate incident with the meatball cannon and an alpaca that ruined my cousin's Bar Mitzvah, and I stopped working on the project. But the facial recognition and contact database software worked swimmingly."

Alex zoomed in on the face of the man in the lab coat. "Excuse me, Ms. Brinkles. I've got a phone call to make."

* * *

The Casa Del Cucaracha Motel's sign fizzled and blinked, casting a flashing, neon letter U through the motel window and across Dr. Thorium's room.

Still wearing his torn, burned lab coat, Thorium leaned back against the headboard and massaged his temples. The red "TL" logo lay near the door. He'd torn it off the coat a few hours ago.

The room smelled like cigarettes and shame, and the green stains on the ceiling and walls suggested someone had set off a relish bomb. And he could've sworn he'd seen a rat the size of a Bichon Frisé in the bathtub.

Thorium wasn't in great shape, either. He hadn't shaved or showered in days. He sipped lukewarm water from a Styrofoam cup.

The police questioning had gone better than he'd expected. After he'd recovered from Lil' Poochy's attack, the police station's medic had bandaged him up, and he'd been taken in for questioning.

Dr. Thorium hadn't lied to the cops. After all, he was no criminal or "mad scientist." He'd simply left out a bit of information.

He'd told the cops that he was a scientist working within the constraints of an independent budget. He told them Lil' Poochy had attacked him, taken over his lab, and dragged him to the police station before releasing the Birthday Gang.

Thorium sat up and stared at the Styrofoam cup. He hadn't lied. He was worried about being assaulted again, so he'd told the cops he couldn't remember where the lab was. Which was true enough. After all, it wasn't a lab anymore. And he'd told the cops he'd never seen Lil' Poochy before. Which was true enough. His little Floofles was gone, and that silver-suited monster had taken his place.

The ringing of the phone pierced the silence. Thorium groaned. It must be the cops or those lobster-munching corporate bigwigs who'd rejected his ideas.

He pulled the phone out of his pocket and looked at the screen, but there was no name or number. Instead, the image of a walrus head against a white background filled the screen, a logo with a black head and tusks, a blue muzzle, and piercing, blue eyes.

Could it be? His finger trembling, he answered the call.

"Hello?"

"Doctor Filbert Thorium?" said a familiar voice.

"Who wants to know?"

"You're no fool, Thorium. You know who this is."

Dr. Thorium stood and paced around the motel room. "What do you want? To rub my nose in my failures? Just like everyone else?"

"Enough of your mopiness! I know you've seen Lil' Poochy's broadcast. He's endangering the lives of dozens of innocents. You're as smart as a juggling marmoset in circus pants among a gaggle of regular marmosets.

"You built a jetpack and harness device into a dog collar, for vibrissae's sake. I'm sure you've installed some kind of tracking device on Lil' Poochy."

Thorium cleared his throat. "So what if I have? Why would I help you locate my former pet?"

"Revenge," said the voice on the other end. "And decency. You're not a mad scientist, Dr. Thorium."

The dejected chemist stopped pacing. "You told me when we fought in the middle of the street that you wanted to help Cremini City," the voice continued. "If you can stop it, you won't let a bunch of widows and orphans and kittens explode."

Making one of his hands into a fist and placing it on his hip, Dr. Thorium raised his head and looked through the stained window at the evening stars.

The Black Walrus did have some pretty impressive devices, like the program he was currently using to block his phone number and project his logo onto the screen. Maybe Thorium could still advance the cause of science in Cremini City, just in a more indirect way....

"There is a tracking device," he said at last. "Would you prefer that I send you the coordinates by text? I can encrypt the message."

* * *

The Black Walrus grinned as a new window popped up on the computer screen, this one with a bunch of encrypted gibberish. His fingers drilled the keyboard. Stevia heard him mutter beneath his breath, something about how long the computer was taking to decipher the message and how long it would take to get to the warehouse district.

At last, an address appeared on the screen. At the Black Walrus' bidding, the computer screen flipped through a few windows until the screen showed the series of blue cubes again.

It was a three-dimensional map of the warehouse district! One of the hundreds of rectangular shapes flashed red. "There's our nefarious canine's hideout," Alex remarked, pointing at the screen.

"Then our clump of baked potatoes is fully-loaded, my friend," Stevia said, eyeing the walrus Alex sat on as its big, black eyes stared back at her. "So how are we getting in? I don't expect a welcoming committee, and the Birthday Gang probably won't be as easy to take down as they were last time."

"That they won't, my gherkin-popping chum. But I won't be going in alone."

"I know, but I'm no fighter. I don't think I'll be able to—"

"I wasn't talking about you."

The Black Walrus turned around and stood from his walrus seat, facing the rear of the cave. Reaching to his chest, he fiddled with the wiring beneath his walrus-muzzle-shaped chest piece.

"What are you doing?" Stevia asked.

"Learning to communicate."

A series of blips emanated from the chest piece and echoed through the cave. Each walrus twisted its head to face Alex.

A slow, floppy stampede, the marine mammals woke from their naps and hoisted themselves out of the pools with their tusks, shuffling on their fins to the middle of the cave until they all stood before Alex, eagerly looking to the Black Walrus, a pinniped army awaiting its general's command.

Chapter 24

Gary shivered. The cool night air whistled through the open window and rippled across his skin. He tried to keep his eyes on what he was doing, but he kept glancing at the party popper pistol resting on the table.

His purple party hat bumped against the single, exposed light bulb that hung over the card table, and the dim light made it difficult to make out the objects in the room's corners. More than once, Gary could've sworn he saw a figure in spandex and a black mask.

"Gary!"

"Huh?"

"You gonna call or fold or what, man?"

"Oh, yeah. Sorry. I, uh ... I call."

Gary turned his attention back to his cards and snapped the band of his party hat against his chin to keep himself alert.

Lil' Poochy had put him and a few others on lookout duty in the guardhouse in front of the main warehouse. The guardhouse was kind of big for a security building, but that made it more comfortable, which was fine with Gary.

He and the boys had found a deck of cards in a file cabinet. They'd all set their weapons on the table, within easy reach, of course.

A tiny black-and-white TV buzzed on top of the file cabinet in the corner. No reports of the Black Walrus outing himself to the news media yet, but Lil' Poochy had assured them it would happen.

They continued their poker game. Stan dealt out more cards, and the next round of betting began. Eddie opened. Jack folded and tossed his cards across the table. Ricky raised.

Gary sighed and scratched his head, tilting his party hat to one side. He stared at his cards and the tempting pot of poker chips on the table and the popper pistol ready for action and the smooth, brown bump rising up between Stan and Eddie ....

Like the rising sun over a field of grain, the blubbery face of a walrus slowly crested above the table. Its black eyes were locked onto Gary.

The walrus blew out of its nose, tussling its whiskers as the gangsters exchanged concerned glances and reached for their weapons. In one motion, Stan grabbed his popper pistol and whirled it toward the walrus.

With a deft slap, the blubbery sea mammal swatted Stan across the face, sending him straight into the table and scattering the poker chips. Stan's pistol fired, sending a confetti shot harmlessly into the wall. Jack reached into his party favor bag and pulled out a cake knife, but something smacked him in the back of the head.

He turned just in time to be pelted by a barrage of wet fish. The torrent of trout hit Jack so hard he flew across the guard house and smacked against the wall, blacking out.

Another walrus, this one wearing a satchel full of fish, hopped through the window and plopped on top of Eddie, who yelped and grappled for his confetti cannon but couldn't reach it. The walrus clapped its fins together and bellowed triumphantly.

Gary grabbed his own popper pistol. His hands shaking, he pointed it at the walrus on top of Eddie and took aim for its head.

But he'd forgotten about the first walrus, the one who'd slapped Stan. Planting its tusks into the floor, the creature hoisted itself into the air and flipped forward, bringing its tail down on Gary's head with a thwack. Gary felt the pistol slip through his fingers, and everything went dark.

* * *

A series of blubbery grunts and growls came over his earpiece radio. The Black Walrus nodded.

"Understood. The guardhouse is clear. Excellent work, Jorge. Hold your position with Maureen and let me know if anyone leaves the warehouse itself. Keep a firm tusk and a bristly muzzle, my friend. The rest of us are going in."

The Black Walrus stood outside one of the windows on the first floor of the warehouse. Sneaking up on this place had been as easy as bouncing quarters off a bald man's head.

As he'd suspected, Lil' Poochy and his cronies hadn't had time to activate the warehouse's security system, so none of the cameras were on. Alex just had to move quietly, his specialty. After all, he'd baked a legion of tuna soufflés last Arbor Day, and not one of them had collapsed.

Alex peered inside one of the warehouse's windows and adjusted the lenses of his mask to accommodate the dark interior of the warehouse. He spotted the heat signatures of a few members of the Birthday Gang patrolling the first floor.

He checked his wrist and swallowed hard. Only seventeen minutes until Lil' Poochy launched the missile.

Twisting one of the tusks on the front of his uniform, he activated the communications scrambler. The gang wouldn't notice at first, but any cell phones, walkie-talkies, or radios they had were now useless.

He heard the ding of an alert as he received another call over his earpiece radio, which was immune to his signal-jamming technology. He placed his finger against the side of the mask to activate the radio. "Yes, Ms. Brinkles?"

"Hey, can we go over the plan again? I had a little brine in my ears the first time you explained it."

"Sure. The warehouse has three floors," Alex explained in as low a whisper as he could muster. A guard had stepped a little too close to his window. "That diabolical doggie chose his hideout well. There aren't any windows on the second floor and only one on the third.

"Lil' Poochy plans to launch the missile out of the third-floor window. I could use my grapple gun to zip straight to the third-floor window, but if I do that, the nasty mutt will see me coming and launch the missile. We have no choice but to enter on the first floor.

"Most of the Birthday Gang is patrolling the first floor to take care of intruders. I need you and the walruses to distract the guards while I, like a wispy, silent fart of shadow escaping the buttocks unseen, prowl to the upper floors and face the forces of injustice therein."

A pickle crunched over the radio, "10-4, mi compadre. I'll wait for Fabio's signal."

From the other side of the warehouse, Alex heard Fabio's mighty walrus bellow. The smash of glass told him that the first wave of walruses had entered.

Alex slipped his fingers beneath the opening at the bottom of the window and pried it open. His lenses showed him the outlines of party-garbed gangsters rushing all over the warehouse.

His approach masked by the chorus of belches, barks, and Ms. Brinkles' cries of "Choke thee upon the dills of my fury!", he slipped through the window and clung to the wall, keeping himself hidden in the shadows.

All around him, walruses used their blubbery fins and tails to slap and smack the Birthday Gang like they were crime piñatas. One of Lil' Poochy's henchmen darted from behind a stack of crates just a few feet from Alex, balancing a plate of cake in one hand and holding a party popper pistol in the other.

Just before the fiend saw the Black Walrus, Harriet raised herself up on her flippers and flopped in front of the sinister partygoer. He leveled his weapon at her blubbery face, but she deflected the barrel and opened her huge walrus maw, bellowing in the man's face and hitting him with a blast of fish breath. He fell like an oak.

To his left, Alex saw an ice cream-wielding fiend fall beneath Jerome's mighty tail. He felt the unconscious gangster's cheek brush against his left boot as the thug hit the ground.

Alex's hiding spot by the window was getting too crowded. Seeing an opening between his blubbery allies, the Black Walrus dashed forward, his cape bobbing like an over-caffeinated manta ray.

As he hopped between the crates that littered the warehouse floor and around the mobsters locked in combat with his walrus brigade, Alex scanned the massive room for a way to the second floor. Though he couldn't see the stairs, he knew they'd be crawling with guards. There had to be another way up.

Then he saw it, like a dirty, metal beacon from the heavens: an air vent on the far side of the room. He could crawl through the ventilation system to get to the next floor.

One of the guards smacked a walrus with a balloon baton and shined a flashlight straight toward Alex. Alex ducked beneath the beam of light and somersaulted toward the criminal. Springing upward as he stood, he punched the gangster in the jaw.

No sooner had the brightly colored henchman hit the ground than the Black Walrus heard the snick of two popper pistols being loaded behind him.

Chapter 25

"Well, ain't this a fine candle to stick in our cake," said a Birthday Gang hoodlum as he strode to the front of the Black Walrus while his companion covered Alex's back. "We figured you'd be down at the news station turning yourself in. But I guess after that stunt in the alleyway, we should've learned to expect the unexpected."

He took another step forward, aiming his party popper pistol just beneath the Black Walrus' chin. "You remember kicking me in the head back in the alley? No, of course you don't. We're just peons to you, little action figures you use to play hero.

"But now, no one can stop us from having our way with this city. Not the cops and certainly not some weirdo in blue spandex who plays with grappling hooks. Just who do you think you are, anyway?"

Alex grinned. He'd been hoping someone would set him up for a one-liner. "I am the spoon of truth that roots out the fruit of corruption from the bottom of society's yogurt."

With one swift motion, the Black Walrus grabbed the barrel of the party pistol that was pointed at his chin and shoved it away, just as the gangster fired. Then, glancing behind him, he reached to his utility belt and lodged a blubber pellet in the pistol barrel pointed at the back of his head.

The gangster behind Alex pulled the trigger, not realizing there was a blubber pellet stuck in the end of his pistol. The pellet burst, and a yellow, gooey substance splattered all over his weapon.

Alex punched out the man in front of him, then whisked the blubber detonator out of its belt pouch, pressing the button. The blubber exploded, sending the other criminal stooge flying across the warehouse.

The Black Walrus glanced around the room. Taking down criminals was almost as satisfying as his weekly mustard and calamari bath, but he'd given away his position.

He sprinted for the vent as hoodlums clad in party hats took aim from every angle. Razor-edged confetti, throwing knives, and cake slicers ricocheted off the warehouse floor as Alex ducked and dashed all over the room, making himself as difficult to hit as he could. There was only one way to get to the vent now.

Reaching into the folds of his cape, he grabbed two fistfuls of smoke bombs and tossed them in all directions. Clouds of purplish smoke erupted all around him.

Alex activated his mask's thermal imaging. The gangsters and walruses coughed and sputtered and bellowed. He knew the vent was straight in front of him and threaded his way between gangsters and walruses alike as he maneuvered toward it.

He glanced at his wrist. Eleven minutes. He grimaced. The smoke bombs made a good distraction, but he needed a faster way to reach the vent and the second floor.

Through the smog, Alex caught sight of a familiar, blubbery silhouette. This was his chance.

"Tobias," he shouted, "Maneuver 2319. Quickly."

A walrus waddled out of the purplish smoke and planted his left flipper on the concrete floor. He pivoted around the flipper, his body sliding like a curling stone, until his back faced Alex. Alex drew one of his grapple guns.

Like he was mounting a flabby staircase, he ascended Tobias' back and vaulted off his head. He was above the smoke now and could see the ceiling. The Black Walrus raised the grapple gun and took aim at one of the light fixtures hanging between he and the vent.

The grappling hook wound around the light. The Black Walrus swung toward the vent like a bicyclist Tarzan. He picked up speed, and air whooshed past him. His cape billowed.

As he neared the vent, he spotted something out of the corner of his eye: a hole in the smoke. A hole in the smoke with a confetti cannon and a glistening, bedazzled "party time" tee shirt in it!

The party-themed fiend straightened his balloon hat and took aim at Alex's delicate cranium. Even from this distance, the Black Walrus could see the gangster's yellowed, crooked, sneering teeth. The henchman's finger reached for the trigger.

With a smash, a pickle jar broke against the gangster's head, and a hail of tiny pickles struck him in the chest like they'd been fired from a machine gun, sending him stumbling back into the smoke cloud.

As he soared across the warehouse, Alex heard a shout: "I don't sacrifice my gherkins for just anyone, kid. Go put that Chihuahua in the doghouse!"

Alex landed on the warehouse floor in front of the opposite wall, his cape folding over his legs as he bent his knees. The vent was directly above him now.

A blindfolded figure leapt from the shadows: Piñata Pete! The candy-crazed thug drew his baseball bat and smacked the cement floor. A sizeable piñata was strapped to his back.

The Black Walrus had avoided most of the Birthday Gang by obscuring their sight, but he realized that didn't present a problem to the man who always wore a blindfold. Pete leapt toward Alex, swinging his bat like a meat cleaver while the Black Walrus bounded out of the way.

"Gotta say, I admire your nerve, kid," Pete said as he took another swing at Alex's head. "Not just anyone would risk the lives of a bunch of orphaned kids and kittens to take down a couple of low-life criminals. You sure you want to mess with the Birthday Gang again?"

The Black Walrus ducked and struck the goon in the stomach with a quick punch. "Your mind games won't save you, villain. Against the forces of good, you are but a pair of quadruple amputees in a three-legged race."

Alex swept his leg beneath Pete, but his opponent hopped over it and jabbed at Alex with the bat, trying to hit him in the sternum.

Twisting to his left, the Black Walrus grabbed the end of the baseball bat and thrust it upward, hitting Pete on the chin. Alex tossed the bat aside as the blindfolded menace staggered back and drew the piñata from behind his back.

He grabbed a metal handle and racked the piñata's mechanics, preparing to fire. The colorful, papier-mâché donkey opened its mouth, revealing a steel barrel.

"Whatever you say, Walrus. I was just trying to save some poor sap from having to clean your candy-coated corpse off the warehouse floor."

Pete pulled the piñata's trigger, and a spray of rapid-fire candy flew toward the Black Walrus. Alex jumped behind a stack of crates as lollipops, candy rolls, little pieces of gum, and fun-sized candy bars blasted through the wood of the crate and the folds of his cape, barely missing his body.

He dodged from one crate to another as ballistic bonbons and wooden splinters filled the air. Taking cover behind the crates wasn't doing him much good. Pete's chuckling grated against Alex's nerves like a backscratcher against an ostrich with eczema.

As Alex gritted his teeth and ducked behind yet another crate, his eyebrows popped up. Even though it'd been converted to a machine gun, there was a good chance Pete's weapon was, in many ways, still a piñata.

Peeking from the edge of the crate, Alex spotted the baseball bat lying on the ground. He took a deep breath. He'd need to do this in one motion.

The Black Walrus dove toward the baseball bat, reaching for it with his right hand while his left gripped the grapple gun on his utility belt. He grabbed the bat, and just before he hit the ground, drew the gun, aimed for Pete's leg, and fired.

The hook and grapple line sailed toward the fiend's leg like a hungry snake toward a cylinder of saltwater taffy.

The line wrapped around Pete's leg, yanked him off his feet, and dragged him across the concrete floor and toward the Black Walrus. Just before Pete reached him, Alex whirled the baseball bat in an arc like he was swinging a golf club.

The bat smashed against the piñata-based weapon, shattering the papier-mâché and sending a spray of candy into Piñata Pete's face. Before the blindfolded ruffian could react, the Black Walrus smacked him on the head, knocking him out.

Alex nodded and dropped the baseball bat. Snuffling and slurping sounded from behind him as walruses sucked pieces of candy from the warehouse floor. He looked at his wrist. Eight minutes.

He retracted the grapple line and shot again, this time hitting a light fixture just above the vent. Alex zipped up to the vent, tore off the grating, and dove into the opening.

Chapter 26

On the second floor of the warehouse, Felix Cumpleaños crept between the empty crates and occasional rats' nests, confetti cannon at the ready. The florescent lights were on, but dimmed, and it was difficult to make out the shapes of the crates that surrounded him.

Dust clogged his sinuses. The only sounds were the clack of his dress shoes against the cement floor.

He pulled out his radio and tried once again to get an update on the situation downstairs. Nothing but static. Felix stared at the radio for a moment but quickly shook his head and put it away. The piece of junk must've had a bad battery. That was all.

Crouching, he rounded a corner for the fifteenth time as he scoured the same area. Someone was there!

Felix flinched as he almost ran into what he could've sworn was a figure clad in blue spandex and a black cape.

"Jeez, Tim," he said, lowering his weapon as he panted. "Let me know you're coming next time. I thought you were the Black Walrus."

Snickering, Tim adjusted his paper crown and put one of his thumbs beneath his "birthday boy" bib like it was a pair of overalls.

"The Walrus? Felix, you know he's not gonna show. I'm sure he's on the news outing himself. He's some store owner we shook down or a rogue cop, probably."

A soft ping, like a nail dropping on a metal floor, caused Felix to glance behind him. Nothing was there. Tim put his hand on his boss' shoulder. "You're just shaken up from the last time we encountered the Black Walrus, that's all. We're just here as a precaution, man. And if Lil' Poochy wants to pay us to stand around an empty warehouse, I'm not gonna complain."

Felix removed his fedora and fanned his face with it. "I'm not so sure. The city's changing. I'm starting to think knives and guns are no match for spandex and fancy one-liners."

For a moment, Felix thought he saw a cape disappear between some crates. He darted behind Tim and raised his cannon.

"I just saw something, Tim. It went between those two boxes."

Tim turned and walked behind Felix's back toward the other side of the second floor. "Come on, Felix. You used to be our leader, for wrapping paper's sake. You can't get jumpy every time—"

A clunk interrupted Tim, and he fell silent. Beads of sweat pooled beneath the brim of the gang leader's hat. He smelled something … smoky.

As he peered at the floor, Felix saw a thick smoke cloud pool around his feet, hiding his dress shoes completely and spreading throughout the rest of the room. Swallowing the lump in his throat, Felix whipped around and fired.

A blast of sparks and confetti tore through the air as Felix stared straight into the face of … nothing. Tim's body was there, lying unconscious in the cloud of smoke that blanketed the floor, but Felix saw nothing else in the darkness.

As he knelt and felt around in the fog, Felix grabbed hold of something hard, but wobbly. Lifting some bumpy, plastic device toward his face, he squinted to examine it in the darkness. It had an oversized top, and there was some sort of goo dripping from it.

In fact, it looked like ... a bobble head. A walrus bobble head. With ... lotion oozing from the eyes? Again, he felt the floor. Lotion. This thing had coated the floor in lotion, causing Tim to slip and knock himself out on the concrete.

Felix heard what sounded like boots landing on cement to his left. He spun around, firing four more times. With a loud "tink, tink, tink, tink," four more blasts pinged off the opposite wall as Felix glared into blackness once again.

His palms and the trigger of his cannon were getting sweaty, and Felix felt on his cheeks the cold haze of the smoke, which grew thicker by the minute.

Circling Tim and jerking his head around to see in every direction, Felix felt like his stomach was full of cold stones. A hundred shadows and shapes, accentuated by the dim florescent light, played with his mind.

But there was nothing. No sight or sound of the Black Walrus.

Finally, he fired three times into the air and yelled: "Where are you, you miserable piece of cake?!"

As if in answer, a billowing, cape-like shadow flew through the fog like a vengeful phantom, coming straight toward the gangster. Felix fired seven more times, but his shaking hands caused the shots to fly harmlessly into the walls.

Felix tried to fire again, but his cannon clicked. He was out of ammo. The specter drew closer. The folds of its cape flapped furiously as the mask lenses stared into Felix's eyes. There was only one thing to do.

Wiping his sweaty hand on his overcoat, Felix drew his knife and set a scowl on his face. With a shout, he charged forward and plunged his knife straight into ... a cape?

It was just a cape. Felix ran his hand across the black fabric hanging off his knife until his fingers touched a golden hook connected to a familiar-looking cable. A cable that could have been used to—

* * *

With a kick to the head, Alex knocked out the Birthday Gang's leader. It felt strange to take on a criminal without his cape and cowl, but he'd needed them for something else.

He retracted the grappling line, which he'd slung through a series of openings in the vents like a pulley, and slipped the cape and cowl back on. After he retrieved his boots, which he'd tossed across the room to distract Felix, he was once again suited-up.

It'd taken Alex a while to sneak through the vent system and rig his cape like a marionette. He peeked at his wrist and groaned. Only a minute-and-a-half until launch time.

Alex spied the stairs leading to the third floor of the warehouse. A beam of light emanating from the top of the staircase told Cremini City's defender that, unlike the rest of the warehouse, the top floor was well-lit and hard to access without using the staircase or entering through its single window. That's why, Alex guessed, Lil' Poochy had chosen this warehouse as his headquarters.

Alex was sure there were vents and air ducts on the third floor and that he could find some shadows to slink into to hide himself from the villainous pup. But stealth took time—time he didn't have.

Alex breathed out through his nose. The only way to make it to Lil' Poochy in time was to make himself as obvious as a break-dancer among Buckingham Palace guards. He had no choice. He bounded up the stairs to confront his furry nemesis.

Chapter 27

The bright lights of the upper floor struck Alex in the face like his eyes were belly-flopping into a tub of cold vanilla pudding. He shielded his eyes and blinked, allowing his eyes to adjust to the light. The room was about the size of Alex's living room and kitchen combined.

He spotted a familiar red swivel chair at the end of the room, a large video camera sitting on a tripod, and a missile the size of a koala pointed out the room's only window.

In the chair sat a Chihuahua dressed in a black dress shirt, purple tie, and shiny silver suit jacket. The furry criminal held a reddish brown … cigar? … meat stick? … something that smelled like bacon grease in one paw and a remote-control device in the other.

Lil' Poochy peered at a tiny, gold watch on his wrist (or ankle? Alex wasn't sure.) "Well, you have a flare for the dramatic. I'll give you that," the Chihuahua said. "Talk about showing up at the last minute."

He puffed on the meat cigar and hopped down from the chair, sauntering toward Alex on his hind legs and smiling like a shaved alpaca easing into a hot tub.

"So, I finally get to take a gander at the Black Walrus. I've got to admit, it took moxie to show up here. I figured you were just some punk who watched one too many *Super Friends* cartoons as a kid."

The bipedal Chihuahua pointed his meat cigar at Alex like it was an index finger. "But you're the real deal, ain't cha?"

"I am but a servant of justice, a watchful Ranger Smith patrolling the forest." Alex planted his hands on his hips. "And you just stole one too many pic-a-nic baskets."

The Chihuahua chuckled. "That I have. But since you're a 'real deal' hero, I'm betting you aren't willing to continue your crusade at the expense of the inhabitants of the Cremini City Home for Widows, Orphans, and Crippled Kitties."

The black-hearted canine raised his right paw and stroked the missile controller with his paw toes. "I'll give you one more chance: You gonna take off that mask, or do you want to see all those kids in the Home blown into orphan bits?"

Lil' Poochy sucked on his meaty cigar again and blew a smoke ring that stank of ham. It broke against Alex's face. Despite the cool, night breeze wafting in through the open window, Alex's neck grew hot. As he glared at the four-legged crime boss, his fingers curled into fists.

The lenses in his mask began to steam a little. His hands quivered, and he could think of nothing but how much he'd like to dash forward and punt Lil' Poochy to Indonesia.

But the pint-sized canine was right.

Alex sighed. "I just broke into the warehouse because I wanted to experience the rush of crime-fighting one more time, that's all. But my thrilling little escapade is over now. No one's going to die because of me. I assume you can pirate the airwaves again?"

"Of course, m'boy," Lil' Poochy said, trotting to the camera and motioning for Alex to step into the camera's field of view. He pressed the record button and stepped in front of the lens.

"How's things, Cremini City?" he sneered. The malevolent mutt obviously enjoyed showing off his furry mug to thousands of people. "I hope you ladies and germs are ready for a treat, because I've just been visited by our resident hero, the Black Walrus."

"Good evening, citizens," Alex said, trying to sound as stalwart as possible.

"The pinniped avenger showed up just in time to witness the dawning of a new criminal empire," Lil' Poochy continued. "Convenient, ain't it? Now, I don't know about you folks, but I can't think of a better way to kick off a new age of organized crime than to take a peek under the mask of the Black Walrus."

He turned toward the young hero. "What do you say, Walrus?"

Lil' Poochy's tail bobbed back and forth. Alex bowed his head. Reaching under the folds of his mask, he began to peel the black fabric away from his face.

His arm shot from the mask like the jaws of a snapping turtle as he flung a syringe of paralysis toxin at Lil' Poochy and hit him square in the paw, which went limp.

The missile detonator clattered to the cement floor. The Black Walrus whipped out his grapple gun, fired a hook and cable that wrapped around the missile control, and yanked the remote toward him.

Lil' Poochy let out an open-mouthed growl. He tossed the smoldering meat stick out of his good paw and drew a heavy laser pistol as big as his head. With a deafening blast, he split the grapple gun's cable in two and dove for the remote.

Alex reached into the folds of his cape and pulled out two walrus-shaped batons, flinging one at his canine nemesis as he sprinted toward the detonator.

It smacked Lil' Poochy in the face, but not before the dog mobster let off another shot, which hit the concrete just in front of the Black Walrus, scattering cement fragments. Alex stopped short.

Before Lil' Poochy could fire another blast, The Black Walrus dove toward the little dog. With a smack, he hit Lil' Poochy with his palm and grabbed the barrel of the laser pistol, yanking it out of his paws. The force of the slap sent Lil' Poochy skidding across the cement floor.

Chapter 28

Alex tossed the laser pistol away and picked up the missile controller. But there was no time to disassemble the device.

Lil' Poochy was back on his paws and, running on his two rear legs, made a beeline for the red chair. He stood, reached beneath the cushion, and pulled out a tommy gun.

"Eat plasma kibble, you four-flusher!" the Chihuahua shouted as he gripped the tommy gun in his good paw and sprayed a hail of laser fire at the Black Walrus.

Alex bounded in circles, dodging the lasers while still clutching the missile controller. A few shots flew through his cape, and one took a couple hairs off his head. The sparks of lasers hitting concrete seared his boots, and adrenaline rushed through his limbs.

The Black Walrus shook his head. Dodging fire like this, he was nothing more than a cracker in a fat man's bed: it was only a matter of time before he met his doom.

When he remembered who he was fighting, however, a spark of inspiration flashed into his brain.

He leapt to his right, forcing the canine criminal to take a fraction of a second to adjust his aim. Kneeling, Alex flung his second walrus baton at the lens of the camera and smashed it.

Lil' Poochy stopped firing and glanced at the camera, just for a moment. Alex smiled. He'd taken away the little narcissist's audience.

Bounding toward Lil' Poochy like a gazelle trained by Michael Jordan, Alex landed a punch on the Chihuahua's jaw, and he dropped the tommy gun. As the villainous canine fell backward, he grabbed the arm of the chair and pulled himself up, raising his tiny leg and kicking the Black Walrus just under the chin.

In the moment it took Alex to recover, Lil' Poochy chomped on the hand holding the missile controller.

Alex yelped and dropped the device. The controller clattered to the floor. Just before Lil'

Poochy got his paws on it, the Black Walrus kicked it, and it slid across the floor like a hockey puck.

Alex caught his breath, flexing his hand to recover from Lil' Poochy's bite. But neither he nor the Chihuahua mobster removed their eyes from the missile controller. In a flash, the two combatants, side by side, sprinted for the device.

Though Lil' Poochy was surprisingly fast for an anthropomorphic Chihuahua, Alex's Walrus-Fu training paid off, and he was able to outrun the tiny crime boss. As Alex reached for the detonator, now only a few steps away, something smashed against the back of his head.

A fierce pain shot through his skull, and he fell, hitting the concrete. Blinking rapidly, Alex did his best to stay alert. He raised himself on one elbow as Lil' Poochy hopped over him.

"I was going to add that empty bottle to my collection," Lil' Poochy chuckled. "But I guess you never know when something like that will come in handy."

As Alex lifted himself to his feet and rubbed the back of his head, Lil' Poochy dashed ahead and swiped the controller. He turned and faced Alex, stroking the detonator greedily, like a ferret who'd just found the key to a city made of ham.

"You had your chance, Black Walrus," the nefarious pup panted. "But I guess you and the rest of Cremini City will have to learn the hard way that you don't mess with the canine king of crime."

He pressed the button.

A tiny flame burst from the end of the missile. Scrambling like a baby giraffe across hot coals, the Black Walrus bounded to his feet and sped to the missile.

He threw a blubber capsule, which burst against the side of the rocket, covering it in sticky, explosive goo. The flame at the butt of the missile grew larger, and as if it were moving in slow motion, it began to launch.

Just before it flew out the window, Alex reached the missile and slapped his gloved left hand against the blubber. The airborne explosive shot out the window, pulling the Black Walrus along with it.

Alex felt his arm slowly being pulled from its socket as he and the missile soared toward the Home for Widows, Orphans, and Crippled Kittens. The air currents battered his body, and his free arm felt like it was clamped onto his side by an invisible force.

There was no time to fiddle with the blubber detonator and destroy the missile. He flew past the warehouse district in seconds and shot into downtown Cremini City and then into Morels Park, drawing closer to the Home by the millisecond.

Alex felt like he'd left his stomach somewhere in the warehouse district. The wind rushed past him and smacked against his face. The throbbing in the back of his head reminded the Black Walrus that he'd just been walloped by a glass bottle. He felt his consciousness begin to slip away.

His black cowl was plastered to his face; the lenses pressed into the skin around his eyes like cookie cutters. But if it hadn't been for those polarized lenses, Alex's eyes would've been blasted with air, and he would've been completely unable to see.

And he would've missed the tall oak tree on his right speeding closer and closer.

Mt. Porcini loomed in the distance, too. In fact, if Alex looked at the tree from the right vantage point, he could mentally draw a straight line to the mountain behind it. If he could get the angle just right ….

Fighting the wind, the Black Walrus grunted as he drew one of his grapple guns with his free hand. Pulling it out of his utility belt felt like arm wrestling a typhoon.

He took aim at the tree and, taking the air currents and the speed of the missile into account, fired. The cable wound around the tree and yanked Alex and the missile to the right. He'd changed the missile's trajectory!

Flicking his wrist like he was spanking a bad-tempered orangutan, the Black Walrus popped the glove off his left hand, leaving it stuck to the mini-missile.

No longer connected to Alex, the missile soared toward the mountain as the Black Walrus let go of the grapple gun and shot toward the ground. He grabbed the ends of his cape and threw them open, catching the air like his cape was a sail, and glided to safety.

He hit the ground, landing on one knee just in front of a pair of pigeons, who stopped their cooing and grew silent.

In the distance, a fiery explosion blasted against the mountain, sending rock fragments flying off the mountain face and bathing the park in an orange glow.

Chapter 29

"And, after investigating the explosion, police entered the warehouse where they'd seen the missile shoot out the window."

Alex placed his hands behind his head and leaned back against Jorge's lardaceous walrus body as he watched the news broadcast on the Walrus Computer's giant viewscreen. He'd pulled back his cowl to let the cool air of the cave wash over his sweaty face. His arms and legs ached, but after a hard night's work, that was to be expected.

After they'd incapacitated the Birthday Gang, all the walruses had returned to the cave. They now gathered around the screen like children hearing a bedtime story by the fire. And Alex felt like their short, cross-species grandpa overseeing story time.

"The police entered the building to find the Birthday Gang, most of whom were unconscious and disarmed," Max Blatherson continued.

"Their leader, talking dog Lil' Poochy, was apprehended after a brief fight with police. According to the officers at the scene, the confrontation with the Chihuahua likely would've lasted longer had Lil' Poochy not expended most of his plasma ammunition before the police arrived."

On the screen, officers streamed out of the warehouse, each one leading a handcuffed member of the Birthday Gang to a waiting squad car. It was pitch black outside; the scene was illuminated only by streetlamps and the flashing lights of the police cars.

As the camera zoomed in, a group of four policemen walked out of the warehouse dragging a grumbling, cursing Chihuahua by a leash.

Though the cops tried to wave him away, the reporter jammed his microphone in one of the officer's faces. "Can you tell our viewers exactly what happened here tonight?"

"Well sir," the officer stammered, scratching his mustache as his companions loaded Lil'

Poochy into a pet carrier and tossed it into the back of their squad car. "We've gathered a few bits of information from the gang members, and from what I can piece together, the Black Walrus somehow redirected that awful missile harmlessly into Mt. Porcini."

"Any clues about the Black Walrus' true identity?"

Alex leaned forward, rubbing his fingers together. If they were able to deduce that it was him at the warehouse ....

"No. No fingerprints or anything. But I like to think he's just a concerned citizen, like you or me. You know, a guy who enjoys a warm glass of eggnog and dancing a tango with a wallaroo after a hard day ... or is that just me?"

At a loud, wet crunch to their left, Alex and the walruses turned their heads.

"Well, ain't this just sweet as a fresh, baby gherkin," Ms. Brinkles said, wiping her brine-stained fingers against Darlene as the walrus snorted in disgust. "Guess this about wraps up the city's crime problems, eh?"

Alex stood, bouncing off Jorge's stomach like it was a bean bag chair.

"Wrapped up? No, old chum, I'm afraid not. The banana slices of crime are buried so deep within the jello mold of this city, it'll take months—years—to dig them all out. As for tonight, there is but one more thing to do."

"What's that?" Stevia asked, offering Darlene a pickle.

Alex threw the hood back over his eyes. "Heroes are supposed to be selfless, Ms. Brinkles. We are the Rogaine that gives hope to the baldness of the populace. And there are some people I've wronged. I'm not sure what the consequences are going to be, but I have to make this right."

He bolted to the stairway and bounded up the stairs out of the Walrus Cave and back toward the highway.

"Can I watch my Bill Russ Blu-Ray on your big TV?" Stevia shouted after him. But Alex was long gone.

* * *

Wordlessly, Gwen Portobello sat at the kitchen table and stared out the window. Except for the occasional car, the street was quiet. The streetlights illuminated the hedges and trees and driveways of the suburban neighborhood, the same neighborhood Gwen had seen day after day. But she couldn't tear her gaze from the window.

She felt her husband's hand on her shoulder.

"I don't think he's going to come home tonight," Walt said.

"Should we call the police?" Gwen asked, wiping her eyes but keeping her gaze focused on the window. "I mean, he's only been gone for a few hours, but it's so late, and he spends so much time away from home. I'm ... I'm really getting worried."

Walt sat on the other side of the table and folded his hands. "Alex is a good kid. You know that. But even a good kid can be led astray. I mean, where would an eighth-grader go at eleven p.m. on a school night—"

"Mom? Dad?"

Gwen turned her head to see a figure standing in the doorway between the kitchen and the rest of the house, the light of the living room at his back. The brightly lit living room cast a shadow over the figure's face, darkening his form.

He wore a blue, spandex body suit with boots and gloves and a thick, gold belt. Particles of cement and dirt from the boots and gloves collected on the living room carpet.

A squishy chest piece that resembled a walrus' muzzle held in place a pair of tusks and a black cape and hood. The figure stepped into the light of the kitchen and pulled the hood back, revealing a familiar face.

"There's something I need to tell you."

* * *

The next day, at 3:15 p.m., precisely, Alex and Tracy walked out the back door of Cremini City Middle School. The smacks of Tracy's gum chewing beat against Alex's eardrums as squirrels skittered around the bright schoolyard and up and down the oak trees.

The squirrels were gathering every last nut as quickly as they could. Alex noticed their appendages as they carefully darted between the milling students. Such delicate, graceful little legs. In fact ....

"Tracy," Alex said, interrupting his friend, "How much lighting do you think you'd need to make a squirrel discotheque?"

Tracy's mouth hung open, and she almost lost her gum.

"I mean, you wouldn't need much brick and steel to make it, of course," Alex continued. "About one-tenth of what it would take to build a human discotheque. And you wouldn't need huge speakers; small, portable ones would be enough for squirrels to adequately shake their groove things.

"It's the lighting. If we could figure that out, I think those little rodents, with their agile bodies and winter survival instincts, could bring disco back from the grave."

"Alex, what are you ...." Tracy shook her head. Before she could change the subject, a green sedan pulled up.

"I'll see you tomorrow, Tracy," Alex said, hopping into the back seat of the car and waving to his friend. "And I'll see if I can get my hands on the components to make a tiny disco ball."

"Uh ... okay, Alex. Sounds fun."

Alex shut the door, said hello to Mom, laid his backpack on the leather seat, and pulled out one of his notebooks, opening it to a blank page. His pencil flew. The lighted floor would have to be about five square feet, enough to give the little critters room to get funky.

A few retrofitted dancing video games would probably work if he could get the wiring right. Maybe some re-purposed Christmas lights would—

The car turned sharply to the left, and Alex and his school supplies slid across the seat. He bumped against his seat belt and peered out the window.

"This isn't the way home, is it, Mom?"

"No, honey. I wanted to wait until we were out of earshot of your school friends to tell you this, but I spent the day doing some online research on dairy-powered technology."

Alex raised an eyebrow. "Dairy power?"

Mom reached over the seat and handed her son a stack of articles. As he perused the writings, Alex read about the possibilities of cheese-powered ray guns and milk-fueled jetpacks and saw a picture of a cow with four metal tubes hooked to its udders and a plasma cannon on its back.

"Fascinating. Such tasty, calcium-enriched scientific progress. But that doesn't explain where we're going."

The car slowed to a crawl as they turned into the industrial section of town. The rows of houses that made up suburban Cremini City were replaced with tall smokestacks and industrial parks, and Alex smelled more car exhaust than usual.

"I had to dig pretty deep to find that information," Mom said. "I also found out that Questionable Science, Incorporated, just acquired a dairy cow. Now, why would they develop this kind of technology but not announce it to the public?"

Alex's eyes narrowed as they pulled up to the shiny, metallic headquarters of the technology company. "Mother, I smell the egg-fart-like stench of villainy afoot."

Mrs. Portobello smiled. "Your costume's in the trunk."

Sneak Peek!

Turn the page for a sneak peek at the second book in the series, *The Black Walrus and Kevin*!

Chapter 1

Like a featherless, freshly plucked ostrich sprinting out of the scorching, desert heat, Alex dove into a broom closet. He scrambled to catch the brooms, mops, and buckets before they made too much noise; to Alex, the clattering of the janitorial equipment sounded like a clog-dancing sumo wrestler.

He peeked through the tiny opening between the door and the wall. A pair of scientists strode by, pouring over a series of graphs attached to a clipboard and chatting about the "classic rock revival project." Alex sighed with relief. They hadn't noticed him.

Getting inside Questionable Science, Incorporated, had been the easy part. All he'd had to do was throw a blubber pellet at the security camera above the front door.

The small, yellow capsule had burst against the camera lens, covering it in a thick, beige goop. Alex had then dashed in before the door closed behind one of the unsuspecting employees.

Finding information on the mysterious dairy power technology? Not so easy. Questionable Science's headquarters was bigger than his Aunt Gertrude's behind and, if possible, even more dense and inscrutable.

Alex had spent the last half-hour sneaking around the building, keeping himself hidden in the shadows of different labs and offices and eavesdropping on conversations. After all that, he'd learned nothing about the dairy power project Questionable Science was keeping hidden from the public. The project that, Alex was convinced, concealed nefarious intent.

And it was only a matter of time before QS checked their security cameras and found that most of them had been covered in goo.

Alex smacked his gloved fists together. He was frustrated. For a moment, Alex thought of just grabbing one of the scientists and demanding answers. But he rejected that idea like a baby spitting out a spoon-ful of strained asparagus.

Surveillance and information gathering were just as much a part of the job as leaping heroically into the fray with a catchy one-liner. He'd known that from the moment he first donned his costume and became Cremini City's defender.

Alex ran his fingers across the thin whiskers that adorned the brown, walrus-muzzle-shaped chest piece that held his black cape and cowl in place. Each time he zipped up the blue body suit and pulled the mask over his eyes, he took the weight of the citizens' safety on his shoulders.

He was no longer just mild-mannered middle schooler Alex Portobello. He became the Black Walrus, protector of the innocent, bane of evildoers, and the best thing to happen to spandex since the '80s exercise craze.

Alex eased the door open a little and watched the two researchers as they continued down the hallway. He grimaced. The stark, white hallway was precariously narrow, and the florescent lights didn't provide many shadows to hide in.

Still, he had little choice but to follow. He had to gather more info. Poking his head out, the

Black Walrus glanced to either side to make sure no one else was coming down the hallway. He kept low to the ground and crept down the hall as he continued to listen in on the discussion.

"I'm telling you, Pris," one of the researchers said, "once we install the intelligence module into the automaton, we may as well start planning our retirements. Heck, we'll be able to sell the thing for enough cash to fund a thousand retirements."

"You sure it's been tested enough, Craig?" the other one asked. "Artificial intelligence is nothing to toy with. We don't even trust AIs to run government computers. And we're trying to sell one to a music company."

They turned a corner into a nearby laboratory and shut the door behind them. Alex ran to the door, popped open one of the compartments on his utility belt, and whipped out a device he'd completed just a few days ago.

It looked like the end of a stethoscope but was actually a listening device. When placed against a surface, it allowed one to hear noises through walls and doors. Granted, it wasn't quite as impressive as Alex's communications interceptor or explosive blubber compound or head-massaging sombrero, but it had its uses.

The Black Walrus attached the device to the door, and it began broadcasting the scientists' conversation to his earpiece radio. By peeking through the door's small window, Alex saw and heard everything going on the room.

Computers with formulas and graphics flashing across their screens stretched wall to wall. Though he couldn't make out all of the text on the computer screens, Alex noticed that one of them played a video of an old rock concert.

Another pictured complex mathematical formulas that included not just numbers, but the names of different kinds of fried food. In one corner of the lab was a large, vending-machine-looking object with wires strewn about its base. Next to that device was a red lever.

One of the scientists (the one called "Craig") sat in front of one of the computers. "Just think: a legend of rock and roll brought back to life through the miracle of AI technology. Our metal friend there will be worth billions to record companies. Bring him in, Pris."

Pris entered a nearby closet, and she wheeled out a metal table straight out of a Frankenstein movie. Craig picked up some of the wires and plugged them into the mechanical figure strapped to the table. A robot!

Its face, hands, and the top of its chest were made of a shimmering metal alloy. Alex didn't know what the rest of its body was made of because he couldn't see it. The automaton was dressed in a white suit covered in sequins with a high collar and had a thick, bright red scarf around its shoulders.

A dark pair of sunglasses had been welded over the robot's eyes (or maybe the sunglasses were its eyes), and its full head of black, synthetic hair had been styled into a pompadour. Its feet had been coated in a blue leather material, suede probably, and resembled dress shoes.

Each of the scientists pulled on a pair of safety goggles. Craig grabbed the lever on the wall and slammed it down. The electrical device hummed, surging with energy. The mechanized figure jolted on the table as electric bolts flew from its metallic frame. The room's florescent lights flickered, and one of them popped, showering the room with sparks. Then the lights stopped flickering. The whine of the energy surge died down, and the robot sat up.

Craig lifted his safety goggles, a grin plastered on his face, and spoke to the automaton. "Welcome to life, Robot Elvis."

The robot lifted its hand and flexed its new fingers. "Thank you," it said at last. "Thank you very much."

ABOUT THE AUTHOR

Joseph Caldara is a Colorado native and has been writing stories and comic books since he was eight years old. He fell in love with reading as a kid by gobbling up book series like *Captain Underpants*, *Redwall*, and *The Lord of the Rings*. Joseph has worked a variety of "day jobs", including managing financial software and digitizing physical media. In his free time, Joseph loves to play and design tabletop RPGs.

He also really likes walruses. Go figure.

Connect with Joseph Caldara

Thank you for reading my book! I'd love to hear from all of you.

Be sure to check out my website at www.josephcaldara.com.
Here, you can get updates on future books and events and truly engage with the Walrus-verse in all its forms!

You can also contact me via email and follow me on social media and on my video channels:
Email: josephcaldaraauthor@gmail.com
Facebook: facebook.com/Josephcaldaraauthor/
Twitter: twitter.com/joseph_caldara
Instagram: instagram.com/joseph_caldara
Youtube: https://bit.ly/jcaldarayoutube
Rumble: https://bit.ly/jcaldararumble

If you liked *The Black Walrus*, please leave a review on Amazon. The reviews help more people find my book, and I'd love to hear what you think. I read every one of them.